Sum-mit

Sum-mit

The Pistol Murder - A proud farewell
and a peace officers creed

JOSEPH CONWAY

CITIOFBOOKS, INC.
3736 Eubank NE Suite A1
Albuquerque, NM 87111-3579
www.citiofbooks.com
Hotline: 1 (877) 389-2759
Fax: 1 (505) 930-7244

Ordering Information:

Quantity sales. Special discounts are available on quantity purchases by corporations, associations, and others. For details, contact the publisher at the address above.

Printed in the United States of America.

ISBN-13:   Softcover   78-1-963209-78-5
                  Ebook   978-1-963209-79-2

Library of Congress Control Number: 2024903947

CONTENTS

CHAPTER ONE

AFTER THE DUTCH John situation, Craig had gotten a good night's sleep and the morning cup of coffee smelled and sure tasted good. Martha had gotten up before him and the smell of coffee had enticed him to join her in the kitchen. The tranquility was interrupted by the phone ringing. Martha moved to where it hung on the wall and answered it.

"Hello," Craig heard her say. Then there was a pause and she spoke again.

"It's awful early in the mornin," he heard her say. There was another pause, longer this time.

"OK, I'll tell him, goodbye." She returned to the table with an elfish smile on her face.

"Who was that on the phone," Craig asked.

"It was Raul, your friendly commissioner," Martha replied, but she said nothing further.

"Well, what is it that you are supposed to tell me," Craig continued to inquire.

"Raul wanted me to tell you that you are invited to a ceremony this morning at ten o'clock," Martha continued to tease.

"For goodness sake," Craig mouthed under his breath and he took a sip of his coffee. "I don't want to be sitting at any boring ceremony all morning."

"You might want to reconsider that," Martha said looking at him over the top of her coffee cup.

"Would you consider stopping with the teasing"?

"I hope you're ready for this. At ten o'clock this morning there will be the groundbreaking for the new detention center and sheriff's office complex south of Green River." Before she could finish Craig was up and dancing a jig around the table. He pulled Martha out of her chair and did a few waltz steps until she put a stop to it.

"I never thought I would still be in office when this happened," Craig said as he sat back down in his chair. "For this ceremony I'll be glad to sit at however long it takes."

When Craig and Martha arrived at the site, most of the dignitaries were already in their seats. The Mayor of Green River, as well as the Mayor of Rock Springs; the police chiefs of Rock Springs and Green River along with the City Council members of both cities were all seated on the front row of the temporary bleachers that had been set up for the occasion. Craig found a spot on the end of the row next to the police chiefs and sat down.

The ceremony didn't last as long as Craig anticipated. There were several speeches by members of the County Commissioners and a speech by the Mayor of Rock Springs and then members of the City Council. The City Council members of Rock Springs and Green River and Craig were each handed a gold bladed shovel and on cue dug up a shovel full of dirt.

Martha dropped Craig off in front of the county building and he made his way through the long hallway to his office. Now he sat at his desk waiting on the elections commissioner to return his call.

When the phone rang it startled Craig, he was daydreaming, thinking about what he was going to tell the Election Commissioner, Jack Abramoff. He and Jack had probably been with the county longer than anybody and Jack was there when Craig became sheriff.

"Spence here," he said. It was his administrative assistant.

"Sheriff, I have Mr. Abramoff on the line. I'll patch him through."

"Hey, you there Craig"? Jack Asked.

"Yeh you old retard," Craig joked. "How goes it"?

"Retard"? You been in this rat race almost as long as me," Jack came back. "That don't say too much about you either. I left a message for you to call me because you haven't filed yet and this is the last day, I can drop the forms over to you if you want."

"Thanks, ole buddy, but I won't be needing em," Craig said in rejecting offer.

"What do ya mean"? Jack asked rather perplexed.

"I'm going to hang it up. It's time someone else strapped on this bronco. It's been a great ride but like that country singer says, you gotta know when to fold up."

"You serious Craig"? Jack asked with surprise.

"Yes sir Jack," Craig said with some finality. "I'm done. How many people filed"?

"Two," Jack replied. "A guy by the name of Norman Francis and one of your guys, Harry Kushner. I don't know this Francis guy, do you"?

"Yeah," Craig began. "He used to be on the Rock Springs Police Department years back; got run off and took a job as police chief in Hanna Wyoming. When the mines closed, they got rid of the police department in Hanna and had the Sheriff's office do the policing. Does he live in the county"?

"Been in Superior just over a year," Jack advised. "What kind of a guy is he"?

"Let's just say he's not someone that I'd bring on board if I was gonna stick around," Craig said emphatically.

"What you gonna do now," Jack asked.

"We'll probably move out of the county's house the week that the new sheriff is installed, and instead of moving into an apartment we're gonna go to a retirement community. We'll probably travel a bit. I don't have a bucket list, but Martha has some things she'd like to do and see while we can."

"Well good luck to ya Craig. I'll probably stay here till they run me off. Don't have anybody at home anymore so no reason to leave. Say hello to Martha and make sure you come by before you leave. See ya." There was a dial tone before Craig could say goodbye. Instead of

hanging up the receiver Craig pushed the button that connected him to Steve Lolly's office.

"Yeah Boss," Steve answered.

"Got a Minute," Craig asked. "Come visit a bit."

It didn't take Steve long to get to Craigs office. All the way up he wondered to himself what might be up. The Sheriff didn't often call him in unless he had something on his mind. When he entered the office Craig motioned him to sit in one of the chairs at the small conference table and Craig moved over to join him.

"I see you didn't file for this job," Craig began.

"No sir," Steve replied. "I gave it a lot of thought. I've spent a lot of time with you and I know what the job entails. The first year I'd be eating and breathing the job, trying to organize things in the new facility and hiring jail personnel and training them plus making myself available to the county leadership. I decided that the job and trying to raise two teenage girls would not be compatible."

"Are you having trouble with them," Craig asked.

"Not Marla, the oldest one, she's sixteen. The youngest, Milly is another story, she's 13 and a real hand full."

"How's she doing in school," Craig asked.

"Crappy," Steve related.

"How so," Craig continued to prod.

"She' thirteen and about to turn fourteen in a couple of days. She did really well all through the eighth grade and early on in the ninth. Then all of a sudden, things took a nosedive."

"Have you spoken to her teachers"? Craig asked. "What do they have to say"?

"They're dumb as a box of rocks. They think she has a learning disorder and want to put her in special classes. There's something else and I can't get through to her. She won't talk to her sister either. We used to spend time together in the evenings, eat pizza together. No more, she just spends her time in her room or just keeps to herself."

"Sounds like something serious is eating at that little girl," Craig said. "When you first came on board, you couldn't afford a sitter for the girls and Martha used to baby sit them. You think maybe there's enough trust there that she might confide in her"?

"I'm out of ideas boss, I'm willing to try anything," Steve confided. "I'll run it by Martha and see what she thinks," Craig offered.

The Conversation may have gone on, but it was cut short by the phone ringing. Craig was closest to it, so he answered it.

"Spence here," he said. It was Matt Kessler; the Rock Springs police chief.

"There's been a killing sheriff and I think you might want to head up the investigation," Matt said.

"Why me"? Craig asked, a little perturbed.

"It's one of my guys." Came Matts reply.

"Oh crap"! Craig exclaimed as he stood up. "How'd it happen"?

"Don't know," Matt said. "He was found this morning. He was off duty and he was found dead out behind the Crystal Pistol this morning."

"Okay Matt," Craig said. "We'll be right over. Meet me out behind the Pistol." Craig grabbed his hat and turned to Steve.

"Get Kevin and meet me behind the Crystal Pistol. One of Matts men has turned up dead."

The Crystal Pistol was a Bar in downtown Rock Springs on Main Street. It sat among retail stores, lawyer's offices, a barbershop and doctor's offices. It was owned by Paul Mason, a member of the County Emergency Rescue Team and the Sheriff's Posse. Every night after the business day was over the place would be packed with off duty law enforcement officers, attorneys, bank employees, store owners, construction workers and periodically sheep herders that had come to town after being in the high country for six months.

There was a juke box that sat at the far end of the spacious room that always played country western music, and never seemed to lack quarters that kept it going all night. Several rows of tables that sat four filled most of the room. The bar took up one whole side except for a break that provided for traffic using the rest rooms. One side of the break was used to prepare sandwiches and fries and such and the other was for beer and hard liquor. A couple of bartenders and four barmaids kept the place humming until two am every night Tuesday through Saturday.

CHAPTER TWO

BEHIND THE CRYSTAL Pistol was a small parking lot that was used exclusively by the people that worked at the bar. Access was only through a small alley off of "C" street which ran north/south of the bars location. Customers always parked diagonal to the curb on Main street which ran east/west in front. That's where Craig parked and walked around to the alley. The alley was gravel and instinctively Craig took notice of the ground for possible vehicle tracks. There were none that were unique or unusual but there were several. As he came upon the lot there was two cars already there so vehicle tracks would have to be unique to be meaningful.

There was a Rock Springs Police car in the back of the lot, a vehicle parked near the building, and a red jeep in the far corner. Several uniformed officers, two men in civilian clothes that Craig recognized as being "Pappy" Masters and Matt Kessler. The group stood near the back door of the Crystal Pistol. Just to the left of the door, against the wall was something covered with a blanket. Craig assumed that it must be the body. He approached Matt and spoke.

"Matt I'm really sorry that this has happened. I know what this must be doing to ya. I've got my investigative team on the way. Should be here any minute now. Do you have any idea what happened"?

"No Craig," Matt said with a tone of sorrow in his voice. "The bookkeeper comes in early in the morning to take care of the previous night's receipts and she found him over there."

Kevin and Steve walked up and after expressing their condolences to Matt, walked with Pappy Masters over to the body. Kevin lifted one end of the blanket and looked under it. The left arm laid up and over

the head so that the face of the deceased was obscured. Kevin put the blanket as it was, took out his camera and began taking pictures of the scene. He then removed the blanket and took pictures of the corps as it lay.

A visual examination of the body revealed no trauma. When Kevin lifted the arm however, there was some bruising around the eyes and nose. The body was on its right side and Kevin noticed a large pool of blood under the head but there were no open wounds. Coagulated blood on the victims mustache would lead one to believe that the blood ran out of the nose. Then Keven noticed something strange. The victim wore a broad leather belt that was open; there was no buckle. From the size of the belt it probably had been a rodeo type buckle. Kevin spoke to Pappy.

"Can you get the guys over there to spread out and see if they can locate a belt buckle of some kind"?

While the search of the lot was going on Kevin did another look see around the area close to the body and noticed marks that looked like there could have been a scuffle. He took pictures of it and then went back to the body and rolled it over. There was an empty gun holster stuck in the small of the victims back, and it was clipped to his belt. The size of the holster would accommodate a small revolver, *maybe a snub nose of some type,* Kevin thought.

While Kevin made notes of what he had observed, Steve began going through the victims pockets. He removed a wallet from a hip pocket and looked for something that would establish positive identification. The first thing he found was a card certifying that Clinton Tucker was authorized to perform the duties of a law enforcement officer in the state of Wyoming. He also found a driver's license issued to Clinton Tucker. He then put the wallet in a brown paper bag with the intent of closer examining it later. A set of car keys were found in another pocket and what appeared to be house or apartment keys in another.

Kevin finished his initial examination of the body and used his hand-held radio to contact the coroner's office. He then turned to Pappy.

"Can you have one of your people take these car keys and see if they belong to that jeep over there and have them stand by for the coroner while you and I head over to your office and finish up the report"?

"Sure," Pappy agreed. "You go ahead, and I'll meet you there."

The coroner had picked up the body so the entire team, the RSPD leadership and the Sheriff's Office contingent was assembled in a conference room. The mood was somber, and most were busy documenting what they had seen or heard. Craig was the first to speak and his inquiry was directed at the Police chief.

"Matt, how long had the officer been with you"?

"He just completed his second year not too long ago," Matt replied. "He was rather gong hoe. Most of the patrol officers were reluctant to go to a bar disturbance with him because if there was no fight when Tucker arrived there would be after he got there." There was some chuckling around the table and Pappy Masters chimed in.

"He was very caustic in his approach to situations. Even the way he carried himself could cause some people to become combative. When you view his personnel file, you'll see a couple of letters referencing his manner. Lt. Tobias here, was constantly counseling him about his demeanor."

Kevin spent the entire day interviewing members of the patrol division while Steve tried to run down the owner and employees of the Crystal Pistol. Paul Mason, the owner, was south of Rock Springs near the Utah border with the county rescue team searching for a couple of rabbit hunters that hadn't been heard from overnight, so Steve had to call him off. While he was waiting, Steve sat with the bookkeeper, Anne Stoffer, and got the names of all the employees, what their jobs were, and who was on duty the previous night.

Tom Paxton, Lead Bartender & Assistant Manager was on duty; Pete Lomas Bartender, was on duty; Carla Denton, Cocktail Waitress, was on duty; Marta Preston, Cocktail waitress, was on duty; Missy Parker and Dan Denton – Carla's brother – were on duty at the food counter; Max Munson and Mammy Title were on duty in the kitchen. "I'll need copies of their applications," Steve said. "I also would appreciate it if you did not contact anyone regarding this. Is there anyone else that has access to the building"?

"Yes," Anne replied. "The people that clean up the place. They should be coming in pretty soon. They generally clean up in the morning so

that they can get the trash out before the trash truck comes to empty the dumpster."

"Well they won't be able to clean today," Steve advised. "In fact, why don't you give me your set of keys and I'll lock up after I talk to Paul. The place will be closed until we've finished our investigation. After you give me the applications of the employees, including yours, you can go home. I may need to talk to you later if I have questions."

While he waited for Paul, Steve went to his car and got a roll of yellow tape that had **police investigation** imprinted on it and stretched it across the alley entrance and across the frontdoor. He then went back to where the body had been found, where Kevin had chalked the bodies outline, and again looked the area over to make sure they hadn't missed anything, then he went inside and waited.

He had waited close to an hour before he heard someone at the front door. It was Paul and he was surprised to see Steve sitting at a table near the back door.

"What the hell is going on Steve"? Paul asked as he hurried to where Steve was sitting.

"Set down Paul," Steve said. "I'll fill you in. A dead man was found outside the back door this morning. I don't have the coroner's report yet, but it looks like somebody beat up on him. To make things worse, the body was that of a police officer." Steve was watching the expression on Paul's face as he was describing the situation. He saw genuine disbelief.

"Are you shiting me"? Paul said, almost at a whisper.

"Were you in the place last night"? Steve asked.

"Sure, I'm here every night unless I'm out of town," Paul said.

"Did you see officer Tucker in here last night"? Steve asked.

"Yeh, come to think of it," Paul remembered. "I thought it was a little unusual. I've never seen him in here before. He sat right there at the end of the bar pretty much all night. I don't know what time he came in; he was already there when I saw him."

"What time did he leave, do ya know"? Steve asked.

"I left about one thirty, and he was still there then," Paul advised.

"Did he visit or talk to anyone that you remember"? Steve continued to inquire.

"Not that I recall," Paul said. "But I didn't pay much attention to him."

"Was he drinking at all"? Steve continued to press.

"I remember that he had a glass in front of him, but I have no idea what it was," Paul said. "Tom or Pete, the bartenders could tell you."

"Anne was here, she is the one that found him, and I got a list of all your employees from her," Steve began. "I'm gonna have to close you up until we finish processing the scene, probably just for tonight, we should be finished here by tomorrow night."

"Yeah, I get it," Paul agreed.

"By the way," Steve had an afterthought. "What type of crowd was in here last night"?

"It was basically the regular after five crowd," Paul began. "People from the local stores; a few people from the powerplant and mine; a couple of off duty deputies from your office; and a group of about five Basque that were partying pretty good. Most of those people stayed around till closing or pretty close to closing time. When I left, at last call, at one thirty, there was still a good crowd."

"Okay," Steve said, as he stood and gathered the papers that Anne had given him. "Let's lock the place up and I'll check with Kevin to see what else he needs to do here and then get back to you about opening for business."

Steve spent the rest of the morning going over the employee applications, getting phone numbers and address and running the names through the National Crime Information Center (NCIC). Other than a few court appearances for traffic citations there was nothing of interest.

Kevin spent the rest of the morning with several members of the Rock Springs PD meticulously checking every inch of the lot and crime scene looking for anything that might be relevant to the suspicious death of the police officer. While searching a dumpster in a far corner of the lot, one of the officers found a rock. Thinking it odd, he brought it to Kevin's attention, and they noticed that there were two flower containers on each side of the rear door of the building. The dirt was held intact by what appeared to be river rocks. There was a rock missing from the one on the left side of the door where the body had lain. The rock was carefully matched to the empty slot. Close examination of the rock revealed what could be blood, so it was placed in a paper bag to be sent to the lab. Kevin had previously been mainly concerned about what might be a missing weapon from that empty holster on the victims belt Now the rock gave him something else to think about.

CHAPTER THREE

AS THE DAYS went by, and Steve and Kevin were deep into their murder investigation, Craig found himself being amused at the way in which the two candidates for his job were vying for the hearts and minds of the people of Sweetwater County. The county had always been conservative and that was the position of Norm Francis. It appeared that his support was from those who felt that law enforcement was more of a nuisance than a necessity. Norm felt that the current Sheriff did not spend enough time rooting out the sex trade that he felt was pervasive in the county and that the current officers were lacking in experience, modern-day enforcement and investigative techniques. Harry Kushner, on the other hand, came from the persuasion that law enforcement in the county should be conducted on a more efficient metropolitan model. In any case, if he became sheriff, he would pursue the same cooperative efforts between the Sheriff's Office and the City agencies that are practiced now.

Craig tried to stay as far away from the campaigns of each candidate as he could, but no matter how hard he tried he seemed to always somehow get drawn into one or the other. The first instance was when Norm Francis walked into his office one afternoon. Craig was relaxing at his desk.

"The county citizens can feel pretty safe with you on the job Craig." His sarcasm was noticeably ignored.

"As a citizen of Sweetwater County, what can the Sheriff do for you"? Craig asked displaying no enthusiasm or great interest in being accommodating.

"I would think that when someone came to visit your office there would be a little more respect shown," Norm kept prodding.

"Norm," Craig began. "I guess this is as good a time as any to clear the air. I've never liked you, let alone respect you. You were a bad police officer, and should you get elected you'll make a terrible sheriff."

"You didn't feel that way back when you needed help catching that killer," Norm replied.

"Having to ask you for help stuck in my craw," Craig said. "That's how bad I wanted that guy that killed two people and had left another for dead."

"I guess I can forget you supporting me for this job," Norm surmised.

"I would if I were you. In fact you can count on me doing everything I can to see to it that you are not the next Sheriff of Sweetwater County. Now what is it that I can do for you citizen"?

"I've heard from sources that you took money out of the budgets of other county agency's to build that new Law Enforcement and Detention Center south of here," Norm related.

"Oh"? Craig questioned. "You don't say"?

"Stop being coy with me Craig," Norm insisted. "If that's true I'm going to raise holy hell around here."

"Norm," Craig said as he stood and came around to the front of his desk, he stopped remarkably close to Norm. Being shorter Craig had to look up. "First, your sources are ill informed. Second, I don't control the money in this county. Third, you'd best get the hell out of my office before I forget you're a citizen."

Having had the opportunity, though not his usual style, to finally tell Norman what he felt about him, Craig felt like a heavy load had been lifted from his shoulders. No more being politically correct, no more pretending. To celebrate he decided to go visit with some people he liked, Kevin and Steve. He found them both pawing over desks littered with papers.

"You need an excuse to take a break"? He asked as he entered the room. Taking a chair in front of Steve's desk, he took off his hat, used it to clear a spot among the papers and made his announcement. "I just

did what I've always wanted but couldn't." Both Steve and Kevin sat, staring in anticipation. They watched as Craig ran his fingers through his thinning grey hair.

"Well boss," Steve spoke up. "You gonna tell us or do we have to guess"?

"You threw Norm Francis out of your office," Kevin said.

"Dang! Craig exclaimed. "How did you know that"?

"I was leaving the dispatch office when I saw him in the hall heading that way," Kevin said.

"Really boss"? Steve asked. "You know he's gonna be the next sheriff," Steve said with tongue in cheek.

"You think so," Craig replied. "It's going to interesting watching how you two handle that. I have to admit, watching that arrogant SOB with his tail between his legs made my whole day. How you guys doing with the PD case"?

"We've collected all the evidence we could find from the crime scene, processed it and sent it off to the lab," Kevin advised.

"We've interviewed all of the officers that served with Tucker. Basically the information we got coincides with the information you got from the chief and Pappy Masters. We're going through the employee applications now to see who we want to interview and in what order."

"Any idea when we'll get the Coroner's report"? Craig asked.

"We should have gotten it yesterday, but he had to go out of town," Kevin said. "I expect today or tomorrow."

"Have you finished speaking with all the PD staff members that might be able to shed some light on things"? Craig inquired.

"No sir," Kevin spoke up. "I want to spend some time with both Pappy Masters and Lt. Tobias. Pappy because he seems to always have his ear to the ground, and Tobias because he was Tucker' supervisor."

"Since everything around here is slow, I'm going to help Kevin with interviewing those two," Steve advised.

"I know its early Kevin," Craig admitted. "Is your gut saying anything to ya yet"?

"Not a twitch," Keven replied.

"How's things at your house nowadays Steve"? Craig asked.

"Egg shells are beginning to get really noisy," Steve said…

On the day that Steve had mentioned the difficult relationship with his daughter Milly, Craig brought it up while having supper with Martha.

"Steve is having a rough time with Milly," he had said.

"What does that mean"? Martha inquired.

"She's moody, doesn't interact with him and Marla, stays by herself in her room most of the time and is verbally combative."

"How old is Milly now"? Martha asked.

"Just turning Fourteen," Craig replied.

"When I was looking after them, I would have thought Marla would be the one that turned out that way. She was always so independent and stand offish," Martha recalled. "How long has this been going on"?

"Don't really know, but I think most of this school year," Craig answered.

"Her schoolwork is suffering too I'll bet," Martha surmised.

"Steve says it's terrible," related Craig.

"Has he asked Marla what's going on"? Martha asked.

"She's being pretty closed mouth. He doesn't think she'd tell if she knew. He's pretty much at his wits end. Thought maybe you might have some ideas," Craig advised.

"Me"! Exclaimed Martha. "I'm now an expert on teen problems? We didn't have to deal with those types of actions until Katie was in her twenties."

"The girls used to like being with you when you cared for them," Craig recalled. "We were both wondering if there might still be enough trust there that you might be able to get them to talk to you."

"And just how am I supposed to get that to happen"? Martha spoke with some agitation in her voice. Craig just shrugged his shoulders and kept eating.

"Can you explain what you mean about his attitude"? Steve was anxious to learn all he could about Clinton Tucker.

"He was a hard ass," Tobias described Tucker. "To him everybody was a dirt bag. He seemed to have had little respect for anyone that wasn't a cop. I tried really hard to soften him up a little, but I really didn't have much luck."

"How long was he under your supervision"? Steve asked.

"A little over a year. It was a tough year for both of us," Tobias recalled.

"How so"? Steve inquired.

"The majority of our calls are domestic disturbances, Bar related happenings or teenage stuff. Whenever he was given a domestic call, I could count on one or the other of the people involved filing a complaint against him for the way he handled the situation. If he got a bar call, if there wasn't a fight there would be by the time he got through. In fact he and I met the night he was killed. He wanted to talk to me about a write up I had made against him. I had pretty much made up my mind that he was going to cause the department some real trouble someday, so I began to document and counsel."

"What time did the two of you meet"? Steve asked.

"It was about 10:30 that night. I had told him when he called earlier that I had a basketball game to stand security for but that I could meet him after I got through. He said he'd be at the Pistol and asked if I could stop by there on my way in. I told him that I would meet him in front. I pulled up and Parked my unit. He must have been watching because he was at the car before I could shut the engine off."

"What did you guys talk about"? Steve asked as he settled back in his chair.

"He was upset about the letter that I had put in his file. It was really a warning that if he didn't change his ways, I was going to recommend disciplinary action to include termination. We really didn't talk long. He became belligerent and I told him to get out of the car and I went to the PD. That's the last time I saw him until we saw him lying beside that building"…

After listening to Steve relate the story he'd gotten from Tobias, Craig had a couple of questions.

"Was Tobias the last one to see tucker alive"? He asked.

"No", Steve replied. According to Tom Paxton, he served Tucker a drink at last call."

"What was he drinking"? Craig asked. "Did he remember"?

"Vodka Collins with grapefruit juice," Steve recalled. "He also said that he first noticed Clinton about 10:00 or 10:15 that evening. He came in and sat on a stool at the end of the bar. He did leave his seat for a short while. He thought he had gone to the rest room or something. The next thing he knew Tucker was back at the end of the bar and Paul, the other bar tender, was talking to him. Tom said that when he left right after last call, Tucker was still sitting there".

"Was Tucker a regular at the Pistol"? Craig asked.

"According to Tom, that was the first time he remembers him ever being there," Steve said…

It was the last night before his upcoming two days off and Tucker was finishing up his reports after his shift when Lt. Tobias called him into his office. As he entered Lt. Tobias closed the door behind him and motioned him to a seat in front of the desk.

"You went on a disturbance call last night"? the Lt. asked.

"Yes sir, it was my last call of the shift," Tucker said as he removed a small notebook from his breast pocket. "I got the call around 8:15 and I was on scene at 8:27."

"What happened"? Tobias asked.

"Well, when I got there, I could hear loud yelling," Tucker began. "It was a man's voice, and he was cursing and calling some vulgar names. Turns out, he was yelling at his wife. She opened the door and said that her husband had been drinking a lot and she was scared for her and the kids. There were two young'uns, one five years old and the other was eight. When I walked in, he really went off on her for calling the cops and yelling at me to get out of his house."

"Did you call for backup"? Tobias asked.

"Dispatch had a car coming to cover me, but I got there before." Tucker said.

"What's the policy"? The Lt. asked.

"In cases of domestic disturbances, wait for your backup before making contact," Tucker said.

"Go on," Tobias said. "You're in the house, he's still yelling at her, then what happened"?

"I took him down," Tucker related.

"What do you mean, you took him down"? Tobias sought and explanation.

"I put him in a choke hold and took him down," Tucker revealed.

"What's the department policy on choke holds"? Tobias inquired.

"He was a pretty good-sized guy and— Tobias interrupted.

"What is the department policy regarding choke holds, Tucker"? The question was emphatic and insisting an answer.

"To be used only in instances where the officer or others are in eminent danger of serious injury," Tucker answered.

"Were you in any danger at this point"? The Lt. asked. Tucker shook his head indicating that he was not.

"Then what happened"? Tobias pushed on.

"He was struggling, and I was holding on. I guess I held on a little too long, cause he passed out," Tucker said.

"That's pretty much the way Mrs. Burns, the guys wife, laid it out in the complaint she called in against you," the Lt. said as he took a sheet of paper out of desk drawer.

"Officer Tucker," Tobias began. "You violated at least two department policies that you admittedly were aware of. Your approach to the situation was not such that would de-escalate tensions but instead you became part of the problem and nearly caused serious injury to a citizen, who by the way is a veteran suffering from PTSD." Shoving the sheet of paper across the desk in front of tucker, Tobias continued. "That is a letter of reprimand that I intend to put in your file. Read it. If everything is stated correctly, sign it. I've told you before that your

tendency to be physical is going to get somebody hurt. You were lucky that no serious injury happened to that man. Any further occurrences of this sort or any situations in which you cause the escalation of matters and I'll recommend your termination. Is that understood"?

Shocked and dismayed, Tucker's ego was seriously wounded. He considered himself an above average police officer, even though he had been the subject of several counseling sessions during the past year. The words on the page were mostly a blur because his eyes were beginning to fill with tears. He couldn't dispute anything that had been written so he signed it and got up and walked away…

CHAPTER FOUR

STEVE RELATED TO Craig and the rest of the staff, what his plans were regarding additional interviews with Pistol employees, but first he intended to visit with Tucker's mom and see what she may have to offer.

"Sounds like you're going to be pretty busy for the next couple of day's Steve," Craig said as he turned to Kevin.

"What about the Coroner's report, Kevin"?

"I was invited over to watch and take pictures of the autopsy sheriff. It appears that Tucker might have been in a physical altercation at the time of his death. The knuckles on his right hand showed signs of bruising. We're not eliminating the possibility that the bruising might have been caused by the hand striking the ground during a fall but the absence of any gravel or dirt from the area in the skin would support the theory that he might have punched something or someone. Also Tucker did suffer a blow in the area of the upper lip and into the nose. The blow broke the crista galli, which is a thick, smooth triangular piece of bone that projects from the bone that forms the roof of the nasal cavity. Tucker didn't die from the blow to his face however, but one to the back of his head. He Probably sustained that from his head hitting the ground. He suffered a fractured skull which led to a subdural hematoma. The coroner explained that that's bleeding within the skull. He was probably unconscious and never came too. He had been drinking a bit. There was goodly amount of alcohol in his system."

"From what Lt. Tobias had said I would have thought Tucker could take good care of himself," Craig commented.

"Well, maybe he could under most circumstances," Kevin surmised. "The lab found hairs on that rock we sent them, and the coroner matched it to tuckers mustache. So he was probably incapacitated by that blow to the face."

"Have you had a chance to talk to anyone else"? Craig asked Kevin.

"I talked to Pete Lomas, the other bartender," Kevin replied. "He said that he was the last person to leave the bar that night. After last call Tom Paxton cashed out the registers, put the nights receipts in the office safe and left. He said that he cleaned up the bar area and locked up. According to him Tucker left with a few stragglers right at closing time. I intend to talk with the cocktail waitress and the kitchen help over the next couple of days."

"I'll make it a point to stop by your office and get brought up to date," Craig said. "I want to be kept apprised of where you are in this thing. Let's go to work."

Steve had gotten the address of where Tucker was living from the file at the PD. He recognized the street as being in a sparsely settled area north of Rock Springs. Most of the homes out there were mobile homes. He also obtained the name of his mother, Candice Tucker, who was listed as next of kin.

The residence appeared to be a two-bedroom mobile home sitting on a lot that was not well cared for. The home was in need of a coat of paint and a metal shed in the yard had its door missing and was about to collapse. There was a red jeep parked near the shed and Steve remembered that a form for a parking sticker in Tuckers file indicated that he owned a red Jeep.

Steve climbed three steps to the front door and rang the doorbell. From a speaker on the other side of the door a woman's voice crackled through.

"Come on in, the doors open," it said.

The door opened into the living room of the residence. Directly across the room from the door Steve saw a large female on a couch, dressed in what appeared to be a green and yellow moo-moo of sorts. A large hand was wrapped around a big revolver that was resting on an enormous thigh. An oxygen tank stood beside the couch with clear tubing running from it to the lady's face. Steve pointed to the badge on the breast pocket of his sports jacket and introduced himself.

"I'm Deputy Steve Lolly from the County Sheriff's Office," he said hurriedly, still standing with the door opened. "Are you Mrs. Tucker"? He asked.

"It's Miss Tucker," she advised. "Come on in and close that door, you're letting the heat out."

"Sorry Mam," Steve said, closing the door and moving into the room. "Is that thing loaded"? he asked.

"You bet cha boots," she said as she stuck the revolver between the cushions of the couch. "It's hard for me to be getten up to answer the door so I just leave it open and keep old Betsy here close by. What can I do for you son"?

"I'd like to ask you some questions about your son that might help me better understand what happened to him and why," Steve said.

"Don't know that I can help you much. We really didn't visit a whole lot. He worked shifts and when he wasn't working, he was off doing whatever it was that he did."

"Why did he leave his last job"? Steve asked.

"If you're determined to talk, why don't you pull up one of those chairs and sit over here," Miss Tucker suggested. Steve took a chair from a small dining room type table and sat next to the Oxygen tank. "Like I said," Miss Tucker Continued. "We didn't visit much. He came home one evening and said he'd quit his job with the police department and that we were moving to Wyoming. This is the second time we've moved in the last six or seven years. Clinton just seemed to not be able to stay in one place very long."

"Did Clinton have any friends"? Steve asked.

"I'd hear him talking on the phone to people, but I never met any of them," Candice answered. "Once in a while somebody would drive up and he'd go out and talk to them, but they never came in."

"When he talked on the phone, did he ever seem to be angry or anything"? Steve asked.

"Generally I didn't pay any attention," Candice said as she shifted her weight on the couch and grimaced as if she was in pain.

"Can I help you somehow"? Steve offered.

"No, no", Candice declined. "I'm always in a lot of pain. My back, hips and legs hurt all the time. The one thing Clinton did was keep me with my meds to help with the pain. He was supposed to get me some the day it happened."

"Who will get your meds now"? Steve asked.

"I have a daughter," Candice revealed. "I only see her about once every couple of months. She works for the airlines and comes by to see me when she stops over in Salt Lake City. She doesn't know about Clinton yet. Haven't been able to get a hold of her."

"What airline does she work for"? Steve asked. "Maybe we can get a message to her."

"She works for Cloud West. Her name is Tina Morgan," Candice said.

Steve used his handheld radio to contact the dispatcher at the Sheriff's office. He explained the situation and provided the name of the daughter and the airline she worked for. He asked Candice for her phone number and passed it on also. When he had passed on the information he turned back to Candice.

"Do you have a prescription for your medication"? He asked.

"No I don't," was the answer. "I don't remember ever having a prescription. Of course my memory's not that good anymore."

"Alright Miss Tucker," Steve said as he got up from the chair. "I won't bother you anymore right now, but I would like to speak to you again if I think of something," He reached in his shirt pocket and took out a business card and handed it to her. "If you think of anything you

think I should know, please give me a call. When they get ahold of your daughter, the people at the office will call you."

"Thank you. You're such a nice young man. Come by any time. Please excuse me for not seeing you out."

After the movie Martha, Marla and Milly settled in at the Pizza Hut and each ordered a slice of pizza of their choice. They had just seen The Empire Strikes Back and their ears were still ringing.

"How did you like the movie"? Martha asked.

"I liked it," Marla answered through a yawn.

"And you"? Martha directed the question to Milly.

"It was okay," she said. "A little long." As she answered Milly slouched down in the booth so that she was partially lying against the back of the booth and the wall. She was a pretty girl, blond with deep blue eyes that sat in a round moon like face. She was a big girl for her age and shapely.

Marla, on the other hand, was also shapely, but small in stature. She was even shorter than Milly. She too had those deep blue eyes and blond hair, but her face was more angular.

"How is school coming along Milly"? Martha asked.

"Okay." Milly replied.

"Tell the truth," Marla scolded. "You're flunking everything." The pizza that they had ordered arrived and everyone fell silent as they ate. Martha was the first to break the silence.

"I always figured that you were going to really excel in school. You were always so curious and wanted to know about everything. What happened"?

"I don't want to talk about it"! Milly shot back as she straightened up in the seat.

"I've tried to get her to talk to me, but she gets mad every time I try, so I quit asking," Marla said.

Martha took a napkin and wiped the sauce from the pizza off her mouth, leaned across the table and took Milly's hand in hers and spoke very softly.

"When I was growing up," she began. "I would have given my right arm for a sister that I could talk to. I was an only child and I used to pretend that I had a sister and I'd talk to her when I was in my room alone or when I was walking home from school. The only problem was, because she was pretend, she always sounded just like me." Martha paused for a moment still holding Milly's hand in hers, and then she continued. "When I was about your age, I had a really bad time for a while in school. You see, there was this boy. He was the talk of the school. All the girls were gaga about him. His name was Clyde. For some reason he took a liking to me and he was all I could think about, day and night I thought about Clyde. Instead of doing my homework I'd be daydreaming about Clyde. Even in class instead of listening to the teachers I was fantasizing about Clyde. My grades were the pits". Martha paused again as if she were remembering things of long ago. Then she continued. "My Mom was a wise old bird. She figured out what was going on right off. She sat me down and explained the type of life I was headed for if I didn't do well and finish school and that there would be plenty of time for boys— Martha stopped. There was this sound that Milly was making. Her lips were pressed so hard together that they were just two thin lines of flesh and there was this mournful sound coming out of her nose, like-mmmmmhummhumm-and tears were running down her checks and Milly was squeezing Martha's hand. She took a deep breath and blurted out.

"I think I might be pregnant"!! There was a sucking sound as she took a deep breath, and Marla and Martha froze as if time had stopped.

CHAPTER FIVE

CARLA DENTON ARRIVED at Kevin's office as agreed for an interview regarding the night Clinton Tucker died. She was a shapely woman, big breasted, brunette and wore her hair pulled together and allowed to hang over her left shoulder. She was in her mid-thirties and while relatively attractive, the rigors of late nights and alcohol consumption was etched in her face. When Kevin offered her a seat, she moved across the room as if she were in a hurry.

"Thanks for coming in Miss Denton," Kevin said as she seated herself across the table from him. "I hope the timing of our meeting allowed you to get some rest after a long night at the bar."

"Hell I don't need a lot of sleep anymore," she replied. "Between nights at the bar and raising two teenage boys by myself I keep my eyes wide open." Her voice was smooth and light, not at all like that of a person that drinks a lot.

"How long have you worked for Paul"? Kevin inquired.

"Paul bought the place six years ago and I came with it," She said through laughter.

"you been raising those kids alone all that time"? Kevin asked.

"Yeh," she answered. "I was widowed early. My husband didn't come back from Vietnam. We were married right out of high school and he went to work for one of the oil companies. We did really well until the company moved to Montana and we didn't want to go. So Carl, my husband, joined the service. We had two kids by then. He made it through his first tour alright, but they got him on the next one."

"I'm sorry," Kevin consoled.

"It doesn't hurt as much as it used to," Carla lamented. "I've got the kids; they're good boys and they think they're taking care of me." They both had a light chuckle at her comment.

"You were working the night the body was found, is that right"? Kevin began the interview.

"I was working that night," Carla advised. "But I didn't know about it until the next day when Paul called me that the place would be closed."

"Did you maybe talk to him or serve him any drinks that night"? Kevin asked.

"I didn't serve him any drinks," Carla said. "He was at the end of the bar when I'd take a break, I would stand over there and have a quick cigarette. I remember we talked about how loud the crowd was and we laughed about the group of Basque sheep herders that were having a great time. One time when I took a break, he was on the pay phone that's on the wall by the back door. I sat on his stool and when he came back, he thanked me for keeping it warm for him."

"How often had he been at the bar"? Kevin continued to inquire.

"I had never seen him before," Carla said. "He and Pete the bar tender seemed to know each other though. I had no idea he was a cop."

"What makes you think Pete and Clinton knew each other"? Kevin asked.

"Pete was really busy, running around making drinks and stuff," Carla recalled. "At one point I heard this guy you call Clinton ask Pet if he couldn't take a break because he, the cop, had to get home and make sure his mother was alright. I didn't think anything of it then but now when I think of it, that was a little strange that late at night."

"Any idea what time of night that was"? Kevin probed.

"I'm sorry," Carla apologized. "I've got no idea, but it was late."

"What time did you leave that night"? Kevin asked.

"Well let's see," Carla tried to recall. "After last call, I cleaned up the tables that were empty; started encouraging people that were just sipping to drink up so we could clear out by two o'clock; Pete and I took the trash out a little before two; came back in and emptied the place, I would say I left a little after two thirty am."

"Was Clinton still there"? Kevin inquired.

"When Pete and I took the trash out, he went out the back door with us. I assumed he had left." Carla said.

"Was he outside when you went back in"? Kevin probed Carla's memory.

"I really don't recall seeing him," Carla replied.

"Did Pete go back in at the same time you did"? Kevin asked.

"I'm not sure, but I think he was still trying to stuff the dumpster so he could close the lid when I went back in," Carla thought out loud.

Craig always took time each day to review copies of reports from the previous day and night. Generally they were pretty routine; domestic disturbances, drunk and disorderly, bar fights and such. Recently he had taken special interest in the progress that was made with the investigation into the death of the Rock Springs policeman. A copy of Steve's interview with Clintons Mom was in the pile today. As he was scanning through the report something jumped out at him and he went back over the page and read it again.

Miss Tucker was squirming around and had told Steve that she was always in pain. Clinton had always kept her in pain medicine, and he was supposed to get her some the day he died. She also told Steve that she didn't remember ever having a prescription for her meds. Maybe it didn't mean anything, but it struck him as being a little strange. Anyway, he made a note in his notebook that somebody needed to talk to the daughter when she came to town.

Carla had been gone about thirty minutes when Marta Preston, the other cocktail waitress showed up for her interview. Marta was short and stocky. She reminded Kevin of the pictures he'd seen in sports magazines of female soft ball pitchers. She was a dirty blond, and her hair was styled with two large pig tails that hug down her back and ended just below the buttocks. She was dressed in a denim jacket and western styled jeans stuffed in western boots. There was a chain looped from a broad leather belt to a large wallet in her right hip pocket. After

greeting her Kevin showed her to the chair that had been occupied by Carla.

"I'm glad you got my message and agreed to come in today Marta," Kevin said. "It helps me keep this investigation moving along."

"You'll have to excuse me if I seem a little nervous, I've never been questioned by the police before." Marta related.

"I promise you it won't hurt a bit," Kevin said, jokingly. "You were working the night the body was found"?

"Yeh," Marta admitted. "I left early, about eleven fifteen. I needed to pick up my son from the high school. He's on the basketball team."

"Did you see officer Tucker while you were working"? Kevin asked.

"They say he was the guy sitting at the end of the bar," she conveyed to Kevin. "I didn't know him, and I still don't know what he looked like."

"So you had never seen him in the place before, is that right"? Kevin attempted to verify what she was indicating.

"Uh-Uh." Marta grunted.

"You did see a guy sitting at the end of the bar though am I right"? Kevin kept prodding.

"Yeaya, I remember a guy at the end of the bar, I didn't pay any attention to him." Marta related.

"Do you remember when you first noticed him there"? asked Kevin trying to establish a timeline.

"I was getting ready to leave and I went to the office to get my jacket, when I came out, he was there." she said.

"That was about eleven fifteen"? Kevin sought to confirm. "So he would have just gotten there." Kevin said out loud to himself.

"I don't think there's anything else I need from you right now," Kevin surmised. "Could I have your phone number in case I think of other questions"?

"Sorry," Marta apologized. "Didn't pay my bill and its disconnected. I'll be working every night for the next couple of weeks if you need me."

When Craig finished reviewing the reports he sat back in his chair and his mind drifted to what Martha had relayed to him after she had met with the girls, Milly and Marla…

After she had gotten over the shock of what Milly had blurted out, Martha had changed seats with Marla so that she sat next to Milly, who with her hands covering her face was quietly sobbing. Martha had taken her in her arms and let her get it all out. When Milly had control of herself Martha had followed up.

"What makes you think you're pregnant dear"? She asked Milly.

"I had sex," Milly said between sniffles.

"Well, that's how the process generally gets started," Martha started. "However, that doesn't always result in a pregnancy. What makes you think that you have become pregnant"?

"I just feel different." Milly replied.

"you mean you feel different down there or what"? Martha tried to understand. "How long ago has it been that you did the thing"?

"About a three months I think." Milly said.

"And you feel what"? Martha asked.

"I just feel depressed and tired all the time," Milly said. One of the girls who had a baby said that she felt the same way when she became pregnant." Martha let out a sigh of some relief.

"What say we don't jump off a cliff just yet sweetheart," Martha consoled as she handed Milly a napkin to dry her face. "Do you have a study period or a day when you might have a couple free hours for me"?

"Every other day my first class is at ten in the morning," Milly advised. "Like my first class on Tuesday is at Ten. Why"?

"I have a Doctor friend that I'm sure would-be kind enough to put both our stomachs at ease. Have you said anything to the boy"? Martha inquired. Milly began to cry again. "I'm sorry did I say something wrong"?

"It wasn't with one of the boys at school," Milly announced. "It was one of the teachers aids, Jess Preston".

"Oh my God"!! Marla exclaimed. "He's always around the school even when he's not helping out. He's really cute, and all the girls flirt with him. Some people believe that he sells drugs to some of the boys. Milly, you didn't"?

"How did that Happen Milly"? Martha asked, concerned.

"He was assisting Mr. Flannery, our drama teacher, with lighting and stuff when we were practicing for a performance. In the play I am the mistress of this rich man and on that day, Mr. Flannery asked Jess to show me how to come on to the man. After the practice, my job was to put all of the costumes away in the costume closet and while I was there Jess came in. He asked me to show him how I was going to play my part, I did, and I let him kiss me and before I knew it, it had gone too far. We were going at it hot and heavy. Jess put his hands under my skirt and pulled my panties down, Then he leaned me over some boxes and put himself against me from behind. I knew it was wrong, but I didn't want him to stop." Milly had begun to sob again. "Then we heard somebody coming. It was Mr. Flannery. He was dragging one of the scenery panels. If he hadn't been walking backwards he would have caught us."

"How come he didn't see you"? Martha asked.

"He got the panel hung up in the door and was trying to get it loose, so I pulled up my pants and busied myself with the costumes on the rack and Jess went to help Mr. Flannery."

"He's Always hanging around", Marla spoke up. "I wonder how many other girls he's done that to," So this is what's been eaten at you all this time. Why didn't you say something"?

"I was scared," Milly moaned. "Please don't tell Dad. I know he'll be hurt."

"No one's going to tell your Dad until after we visit with the Doctor," Martha assured. "It's been over three months since it happened so she might be able to tell if you're pregnant. If you are, we'll have to tell your dad, because some real problems exist. If you're not, you'll have to set down and let him know what happened and you and he can decide what to do next if anything. Let's take one step at a time. Think you can hold it together until Tuesday Marla"?

"I promise not to say anything. Marla said. "I'm sorry Milly. All this time I thought you were just being a stinker"?

Martha did arrange with her friend to meet and examine Milly. After visiting with her and hearing her story about how things went down, and an examination that embarrassed Milly, the Doctor determined that there was no way that she was pregnant…

Thinking about the way things had turned out, Craig was trying to decide the right time to set with Steve and map out a plan to handle the situation. He knew that they were going to have to take Jess Preston out of circulation, but they would have to consider Milly to. He didn't want to put her through any more emotional stress than she'd already been through.

After the morning briefing, craig had asked Steve to come to his office. Once there Craig started the conversation.

"How are things at home Steve"? Craig asked. Steve leaned over with both elbows on the desk. His face hardened and Craig could tell that he was gritting his teeth.

"I had a talk with Milly yesterday," Steve finally spoke.

"Uh Huh," Craig acknowledged. "how'd it go"? It was obvious to Craig that this was not easy for Steve.

"She said some guy messed with her at school and she had been afraid to tell me," Steve said. "I'm planning on going over to that school".

"And do what"? Craig asked.

"Rip me some ass for allowing it to happen." Steve said and there was anger in his voice.

"Did Milly say who it was that-messed with her"?Craig asked.

"Some boy named Jess, she said." Steve replied.

"And when you find Jess," Craig began. "you're gonna kick his ass, right there in the school, or maybe you'll take a couple of deputies with you, hand cuff him, have the deputies escort him through the halls of the school to a cruiser and drive off with him, lights flashing and siren blaring."

"What are you trying to tell me, Boss"? Steve asked.

"I'm trying to tell you that you have every right to be pissed," Craig said in a fatherly manner. "As a father you should be furious, but this needs a cool head. That's why you don't want you to pursue this. I'm asking you to let me handle it. How is Milly"?

"After she told me," Steve started. "I stomped around the room, yelled and cussed for a while, then we hugged and cried together and then Marla came in the room and the three of us hugged and cried together. I'm glad it was late because I'm sure that I would have gone over to that school last night. Okay boss, you got it, but you have to promise me that at some point I get to see that ass hole face to face".

"Promise." Craig said.

When Kevin got back to his office, two additional persons were waiting. Missy Parker and Dan Denton had responded to a request to be interviewed regarding the death of Clinton Tucker. Missy was a middle-aged woman, that had greyed prematurely and wore her hair in a bun on the left side of her head. She used too much make up and she wore rings of assorted designs on each finger, including the thumbs of both hands. Kevin invited Missy into his office first.

"Sorry for the wait," Kevin apologized. Have you been waiting long"?

"Not too long", Missy said. Her voice was hard and when her heavily painted red lips moved, they reminded Kevin of the cartoon character Miss Piggy.

"As I understand it," Kevin started. "you work on the food counter at the Pistol, is that correct"?

"That's right." Missy said as she admired her jeweled hands.

"Did you work the night the body was found"? Kevin asked.

"Yes sir, but I didn't know anything about it until the next day when Paul called and said we'd be closed," Missy replied. "He told me what had happened".

"Did you know the person who died"? Kevin was beginning to be distracted by the ceiling light being reflected from the jewelry.

"No," Missy said as she cocked her head to one side as if trying to remember. "They said he was sitting at the end of the bar, but lots of people sit at the end of the bar in the course of a night. I don't pay much attention." Kevin reached over and placed his hand on top of hers and stopped the movement.

"What time did you leave that night"? Kevin spoke still holding her hands down.

"We generally shut the counter down at last call," Missy said, easing her hand from under Kevin's and putting them in her lap. "I'm generally out of there ten or fifteen minutes after last call. We don't have anything to clean up and the cocktail girls collect the money, so we don't have to cash out or anything."

"Did you leave out the back door or the front"? Kevin kept prodding.

"I park out back," she said. "I always go out the back."

"Did you see anyone out back in the lot when you left"?

"Just Dan," Missy replied. "He rides with me."

It had been a long time since Craig had been in a school. He remembered the highly polished floors in the hallways, the trophy cases along the walls full of mementos that lauded sport achievements. He had arrived at what must have been class change because the hallways were full of young people, some rushing along, some lollygagging along the walls, some at lockers that were located off the main hallways. He remembered that there were no lockers when he was in school, he carried all his books from one class to the other and teachers were stationed in the halls like sentries and kept everyone moving. What he was seeing was human chaos in motion.

Another thing he was surprised at was the way kids were dressed. Boys in tee shirts that were way too big, and sandals on their feet; those that had shirts on were wearing them open and flapping in the breeze as they hurried along. The girls seemed to be competing to see who could look the sexiest on one hand and others competing to see who could look the most disgusting. He stopped a young lady that looked like she had been hit in the face with a fishing tackle box, and asked her where the principal's office was, and she signaled that he should follow her, he did, and she led him there. He thanked her and she shuffled off in her flip flops.

Craig was greeted by a pleasant grey-haired lady, dressed in a white blouse and blue jeans. The blouse had the name of the school embossed on the breast pocket.

"Good afternoon sir, how can I help you"? She had a smile on her face even as she spoke. Craig removed his hat and laid it on the counter.

"Good after noon ma'am," Craig said. "I'd like to speak with the principle please".

"I'm sorry," she replied. "Mr. Morris is busy right now; can I help you"? Craig casually opened his jacket enough to expose the badge pined to his breast pocket. "Oh, maybe he's not that busy, let me go and get him, and your name is sir"?

"Craig Spence ma'am, Sheriff Craig Spence." he obliged. She left and entered one of the adjoining offices that had a carved wooden sign over the door that said, Principals Office. It didn't take but a short while and she came back with a pudgy gentleman that was almost as wide as he was tall, and she introduced Craig.

"Good after noon sheriff," Mr. Morris had a squeaky voice. "Welcome to our school. I don't believe you've been here before. Could I give you a tour"?

"Nice meeting you Mr. Morris," Craig said in greeting. "Maybe another time. Right now I'd like to speak with you in private."

"Of course," Mr. Morris said as he directed Craig around the counter and led him into his office and closed the door. "Are you here in regards to one of our students Sheriff"?

"I don't think so," Craig answered. "I am here to inquire about someone that is somehow connected to this school. I'm interested in information concerning Jess Preston, are you familiar with him"?

"Yes of course," Morris readily acknowledged. "Jess is a nice young man who got into the wrong crowed and ran afoul of the law. The judge that heard his case elected to give him probation and community service rather than sending him to jail. He is here twice a week assisting our teachers as needed as part of his sentence. He's really a nice young man. May I ask why you are inquiring about him"?

"Sure," Craig said, thinking fast. "His name was mentioned by a person we were interviewing, and we'd like to speak with him to verify things we were told. Is he around today"?

"No, he comes in for two hours tomorrow afternoon. I can let him know you wish to see him."

"I'd rather you don't do that. Could I have his address and I'll stop by and visit with him."

"Yes sir, we have an address card on him. We can make you a copy of it." the principal said.

"That would be great," Craig responded. "And Mr. Morris, I'd like to keep this visit between you and me."

"If you wish Sheriff." Morris assured.

Back at his office, Craig took out a phone book and turned to the map of Rock Springs. The address on the card that Morris had given him was 1225 Doan Avenue He found it in a trailer park east of the city proper. He called dispatch.

"Yes sir, Sheriff." was the response.

"Is SO6 on duty"? Craig asked.

"Yes sir, he's out of his unit right now." he was advised.

"When he comes back on, have him give me a call on the land line." Craig instructed.

Craig was reviewing copies of Kevin's reports on the Tucker case when the phone rang.

"Spence here." he said.

"It's Harry Sheriff, you wanted me to call you"?

"Hi ya, Harry," Craig responded. "How goes it"?

"One day at a time Sheriff, one day at a time." Harry didn't sound too enthusiastic. They chatted a while about the campaign and how it was going and then Craig got down to business.

"I need a job done Harry," Craig revealed. "How would you like to do something to break the monotony"?

"I'd like that," Craig noticed that Harry seemed to perk up a bit. "What cha need"?

"I need you to go over to 1225 Doan Avenue and pick up a young man," Craig related. "I've never seen him so I can't tell you what he looks like. His name is Jess Preston. I want him for questioning pertaining to statutory rape. You might want to have one of the other patrolmen out there with you to provide backup."

"I know this guy," Harry said. "Several months ago I assisted the DEA boys when they arrested him for peddling pills. At his trial, because it was his first offense, the judge gave him probation. Sounds like he could be in real trouble this time. SO9 is on with me today, I'll have him meet me over there."

"Great, let me know when you have him." Craig instructed.

Pete lomas was a mousey sort of guy. He was thin in stature, chiseled facial features with a nose that was very prominent. He was beginning to go bald down the middle of his head of fiery red curly hair. Kevin thanked him for coming in and began the conversation by relating most of what Carla had relayed to him. Then he began his questioning.

"According to Carla, she got the feeling that you knew Clinton Tucker. Did you"?

"Yeah I knew him." Pete admitted.

"How did you come to know officer Tucker"? Kevin inquired.

"He lives out in the same area as me." Pete revealed.

"Were you friends"? Kevin kept at him.

"Not really." Pete said.

"At some point during the night, while officer Tucker was sitting at the end of the bar, he asked you to take a break," Kevin stated. "what was that all about"?

"He needed some pain pills," Pete started. "I suffer from chronic back pain and he knows I always have some."

"Do you always supply him with pain pills"? Kevin asked.

"No, no," Pete said holding up both hands as if to stop Kevin's trend of thought. "I would only give him one or two to hold him over. He had a connection somewhere that he generally got what he needed."

"Did you give him any pills that night"? Kevin asked.

"No," Pete responded. "I was too busy and never got a chance to get away. I didn't take a break all night."

"Did you ever see Officer Tucker leave his seat at the end of the bar"? Kevin wanted to know.

"He left twice that I remember," Pete recalled. "Once early on he went out the front door, I thought he was leaving but he came back and sat down again. Then just before last call he got up and made a phone call."

"When you took the trash out, was Officer Tucker still around"? Kevin wanted to know.

"He went out the back door with Carla and me." Pete confirmed. "Where did he go after he left the building"? Kevin asked as he flipped to a new page on the pad, he was taking notes on.

"There was a car parked down at the far end of the building," Pete said as he looked off as if trying to remember. "I saw him walk toward it, I assumed it was his. I didn't see him get in it; I didn't really think anything of it. There's always somebody parked back there making out and such."

"what was the make of car that was parked there"? Kevin was very interested in what Pete was saying.

"I don't know, didn't pay that much attention." Pete said.

"Was the car still there when you left for the night"?

Kevin asked. Pete paused for a short while before speaking.

"You know, I don't recall. I just got in my car and left." Pete's answer was a little disappointing to Kevin, but he had more information than he had before.

It was close to the end of the workday when the phone on Craig's desk began to ring. It was the dispatcher.

"Spence here." Craig answered.

"Sheriff, SO6 wanted you to know that he has the subject and is heading in." she said.

"Thanks, have him bring the individual to my office." Craig directed. He rearranged the chairs in front of his desk so that Jess would be sitting directly in front of him so that he would be able to stare him right in the eye. He then used the intercom to call Steve.

"Stick around," Craig said when Steve answered. "There's somebody I may want you to meet."

When Harry brought Jess into the office, Jess was cuffed with his hands behind him. It was policy that whenever a person other than another employee of the department was transported, they would be cuffed. Harry was holding onto one arm. Jess was wearing a leather hat with fury flaps hanging over his ears and he was wearing a brown down vest over a brown and white flannel checkered shirt. He had on western cut trousers and brown cowboy boots. There was a tuft of brown hair protruding from under the front of the hat. Craig directed Harry to remove the cuffs and to secure the door behind him. After Harry had left, Craig told Jess to make himself comfortable. Jess removed the hat and unzipped the vest. As Craig looked at him, he remembered that Martha had said that all the girls at school flirted with this guy. Craig had difficulty understanding why. Finally Jess spoke up.

"Sheriff," he said. "Would you please tell me why I'm here"?

"Didn't the officer tell you why you were being picked up"? Craig countered.

"He said you wanted to talk to me about some rape," Jess played ignorant. "I don't know anything about no rape." Craig stared directly into Jess's eyes, which began to dart side to side, trying to avoid that stare.

"Jess," Craig began. "You have the right to remain silent. You are not required to say anything to me at any time or to answer any questions." Craig continued to stare jess in the eye. Jess began to fidget in his chair. "Anything you say can be used against you in court. You have the right to talk to a lawyer for advice before I question you and to have that lawyer with you during questioning. If you can't afford a lawyer and want one, a lawyer can be provided you. Should you decide to talk to me without a lawyer present, you have the right to stop answering questions at any time until you have talked to a lawyer. Do you understand what I'm saying to you"? Craig's stare never wavered.

"I haven't done anything wrong," Jess said, his voice becoming high pitched. "I'm on probation Sheriff, I don't need any trouble."

"Do you understand what I just said"? Craig persisted.

"Yes sir." Jess replied.

"Do you want to talk with me then"? Craig asked.

"I got nothing to hide." Jess said, and he was visibly nervous now.

"How old are you"? Craig asked.

"I'm nineteen," Jess responded. "Be twenty in a couple of months."

"you know Milly Lolly"? Craig noticed an eye quiver at the question. Jess didn't answer right away.

"Well, do you"? Craig pressed.

"Yes sir, I know her." Jess cleared his throat.

"How old is she Jess"? Craig noticed a small bead of perspiration begin to work its way down the side of Jess's face.

"She came on to me Sheriff, I swear she did, I didn't make her do nothing." Jess was beginning to lose color around his lips and Craig hoped he wasn't about to get sick.

"You're a dumby Jess," Craig scolded. "But you're not stupid. You knew if that girl was in that school, she was underage."

"Sheriff, I swear, we didn't really get going," Jess began to beg. "The teacher almost caught us, and I pulled away from her, I didn't really do anything." Now the tears began to flow. "Oh God, I don't need this." Craig sat quietly, letting JESS pull himself together. He then pushed the intercom button to Steve's office. When Steve answered, Craig was inquisitive.

"What are you doing"?

"Just going over some of the interviews with Kevin boss." Steve responded.

"Do you have a minute"? Craig asked. "There's somebody I want you to meet. Can you come to my office"?

"Sure boss. I'll be right up," Steve assured.

When he arrived in Craigs office Steve immediately knew who the person was that sat in front of Craig's desk. He felt the blood heating up in his neck and he knew his face was beginning to turn red. Craig saw it too and spoke firmly.

"Have a seat Steve and let me introduce our guest." After Steve had seated himself at the conference table, some distance from Craigs desk, Craig continued. "This is Jess Preston. Jess has told me that he knows your daughter, Milly." Craig noticed that the color had drained from Jess's face and his breathing was shallow. He recognized that Jess was scared senseless. "Jess here also states that nothing really happened with your daughter, that he pulled away from her when they were almost caught by one of the teachers. He does not deny, that if he didn't almost get caught, that he wouldn't have completed the act. What does Milly tell you about the situation Steve"? Now its Steve that is staring at Jess and it's a good thing that looks can't kill.

"Milly says that he penetrated her," Steve stated. "I have no reason to believe that she would say that to me if it weren't true. Sheriff, I'm pressing charges against this man."

"Jess," Craig said. "I think you need a lawyer. I'm going to arrest you on a charge of Statutory Rape." Craig dialed Sherrie's intercom number and requested that she come escort Jess to booking.

"The jail administrator will come escort you over to booking and you can call a lawyer, or you can request one be provided you and they'll contact the Public Defender's Office for you."

Jess pushed his chair back and stood up. When he turned to face Steve, there was an astonished look on Steve's face. The belt buckle that Jess was wearing was a rodeo type, with the Wyoming logo, a cowboy on a bronc in the middle. The type that Tucker allegedly was known to wear.

CHAPTER SIX

THE **FOLLOWING DAY** for Craig started like most, he and Martha at the kitchen table enjoying coffee together and catching up on the previous day or discussing what was in store for the current one. Martha was in the middle of laying out her plans for the day when she remembered something, she had meant to bring to Craigs attention earlier.

"You remember we were wondering what that construction going on south of town by the river was"? She was saying to Craig.

"Uh, huh," Craig grunted as he took a sip of his coffee. "It looks like some sort of motel or hotel to me."

"you remember that retirement place we went to look at in Thermopolis with Katie"? Martha reflected.

"Yeah, the one by the river," Craig recalled.

"Well, I got a flyer from that place announcing that the company that owns it is opening a retirement home here in Green River," Martha said. "They are taking applications and they plan to have it open for occupancy soon."

"That's a nice location, down by the river," Craig responded. "What are you thinking"?

"I'm going to put in an application. Everyone that applies will be invited to an orientation dinner. The timing is just right." Martha waited to see if Craig would make a comment. "We'll be just about ready to move out of this place and we wouldn't have to leave the area," She continued.

"You know doll," Craig said as he took her hand in his. "That would not be a bad deal. I wouldn't mind that at all."

"I thought you might like the idea of staying in Green River after you retire." Martha patted the back of Craigs hand. "Now you'd better get out of here so that I can get busy about it."

The campaign for County Offices was in full swing and Craig spent as much time as he could with Harry, attended every campaign event that Harry, or the party held. When there was a debate scheduled between the candidates for the Sheriff's Office, Craig spent all of Harry's days off prepping him for what he was certain his opponent would throw at him. He knew that gambling and prostitution would be a major topic of any debate, so Craig made sure that Harry had the most up to date information regarding the Dollar and the current operations. Craig knew that Norm Francis was not up to date on much of what had taken place in the county since he left the police department in Hanna, and the information that he would glean from supporters would be gossip or misinformation.

In all of his interviews with the press and local radio and TV stations, Norm Francis was critical of the current operations of the department and really hammered Craig regarding the lawsuits that plagued the county from the ACLU. This amused Craig because he wasn't running for office and Harry had in no way been involved so he was able to completely avoid having to defend against any legal situations. He was able to speak to progress that had been made in remedying conditions which led to the suites in the first place. Craig also spent many after work hours with Harry, making sure that he understood the relationships that were necessary in order that the politics of the office didn't creep into the departments performance of law enforcement.

On election night, Craig and Martha hosted a dinner at their house and Harry, (the deputy that was running for the job) Sherrie Mullins, Craigs Jail administrator, Steve Lolly and Kevin Marcy, (Craigs second

in command and chief of detectives), all were in attendance. There was an air of nervous anxiety in the room as everyone sat around the TV watching the election results come in. There was some surprise that Norm Francis was leading 1,460 to 1,250 in the vote count. Martha commented that there was a large contingent of fervent religious people, Mormons and Evangelicals, throughout the county and they would be very receptive to Norm's positions on gambling and prostitution. It was early yet, she had cautioned.

As Martha had inferred, as the night wore on the count tightened and then Harry began to edge forward in the count. By 9:00pm Harry was ahead by 132 votes and by 10:00pm Harry had a comfortable lead of 500 votes. There was no way Norm could mount a further challenge. Harry breathed a sigh of relief because he had resigned his position with the Sheriff's department, and he would have to wait six months before he would have been able to reapply to come back.

At the morning staff meeting there was much discussion about the election outcome. All expressed joy that Norm had not succeeded in his quest for the job. When Craig arrived, he had Harry, the sheriff elect in tow. The staff stood and applauded, and there was congratulatory hand shaking and back slapping in celebration of their former colleagues win. After everyone was seated, Craig spoke up.

"It means a lot to me not to be introducing someone who would have no clue about being sheriff of this county. Harry here, though he'll probably change some things to suit his way of thinking, will maintain maturity and civility in this office." Craig paused a moment, reached in his shirt pocket and took out a shiny gold platted badge and pinned it on Harry's shirt, it was a star with six points. Then he continued. "This badge was given to me by the Governor of Wyoming when I was sworn in as sheriff twenty years ago. Across its middle it says, SHERIFF. On each point of the star is a challenge. Respect, Patience, Understanding,

Empathy, Professionalism and Duty. It is these challenges that have guided me in this job. I want you to have it."

Harry spent several minutes thanking Craig and then addressed his staff.

"You all know me; I like to keep this simple but effective. Any changes that are made when I come on board we'll make together. Right now I'd just like to start getting caught up on what the department is involved in. That's one of the reasons I'm here this morning."

"Okay," Craig began. Sherrie, you want to bring us up to date about what's happening in your area"?

"Harry, you may know, or you may not know that the County and this Department were sued by the ACLU," Sherrie started. "As a result, we were restricted as to the number of inmates we could house in this jail. We were required to farm out to locations that met the ALCU standards. We could only hold persons scheduled for court appearances here and once the hearings were over the persons had to be transported back to the alternate location."

"I've made some of those trips," Harry commented.

"Well there is some good news," Just yesterday, and I haven't even had an opportunity to advise you sheriff; we were advised that we can start moving into the new offices at the detention center the middle of next month. We currently have four inmates that will be arraigned today and there are seven being held in other locations. So, I am in the process of planning our move to the new facilities. That's it for me."

"Boy, that is good news", Craig said. "Once you have a plan, give me plenty of time to arrange for equipment and transportation. Well Harry, not only will you have a new job you're going to have a new detention facility."

"How lucky can a guy be, huh"? Harry said, smiling sheepishly.

"Kevin," Craig called. "Want to give us an update on your activities"?

"I'm still up to my elbows in the Tucker thing," Kevin began. "Between the two of us, Steve and myself, we have completed initial interviews. I'm now putting all the information together and determining who I want to talk to again. Also Steve tells me that when Jess Preston was in your office, he noticed that he had a belt buckle similar to the one Clinton Tucker supposedly wore all the time. He's being housed in Evanston and I need to get down there and check it out."

"Yeah, Ok," Craig spoke up. "You can buy those buckles at any curio shop. Unless there is something unique, like initials or a name engraved on it, I'd be careful not to put too much stock in it. I understand that there may have been a gun missing"?

"Yeh, there was an empty holster on his belt when we examined the body," Kevin advised.

"This is your investigation Kevin, and I have confidence that you will do a great job," Craig said. "If you were to ask my advice, which you haven't, I'd say find that gun if there is one, Just saying. By the way, what's with Maggie these days"?

"Nothing but good news sheriff," Kevin said with a smile. "At his arraignment, Ernest pleaded guilty to all charges and is probably looking at two to five years on the assault with a vehicle charge; Five to 10 years on the attempted murder charge; and at least a couple of years on the false imprisonment charge. Sentencing is set for later in the month. Maggie and her attorney was at his arraignment and the judge is the same one that is handling the divorce. Her attorney spoke with the judge and requested that under the circumstances the divorce desired by her client be granted. The judge had the bailiff go get the file, opened the hearing pertaining to the case, asked Ernest if he still intended to contest the divorce, Ernest said no, and the divorce was granted on the spot."....

When leaving the court room Maggie couldn't stop tears from welling up in her eyes. As she dabbed with a tissue, the attorney asked if she was sorry about everything now. Her answer was not surprising.

"Yes and no," she said. "I feel terrible that he probably will go to prison. I know it was his own doing, but I can't help feeling that I played a part in his demise. About the divorce, I'm ecstatic."

The first thing Maggie did after parting with her attorney in the lobby of the courthouse was to locate a pay phone. There were several along the wall near the entrance to the rest rooms. She dialed the number to Kevin's office…

"We're lucky everything has turned out like it did," Craig said. "It could have been so much worse." Craig then turned to Steve. "Steve," he said. "What do you have going"?

"I'm working in two directions, boss. I'm giving Sherrie help with her planning and doing as much of the leg work that I can for Kevin with his investigation. My plan is to go back and visit with officer Tuckers mother and see if I can determine that there was a gun and that it might be missing. Then I'll make the rounds to the pawn shops to eliminate the possibility that it may have been pawned." Craig broke in.

"I get the feeling that you think the shops may play into this."

"Boss, Kevin and I have been kicking this thing around. Whoever took that buckle and maybe the gun wasn't looking for souvenirs. We think they probably were taken to settle a debt."

"Could be," Craig agreed. "If that's the case, I think we're looking for someone in the Cristal Pistol group of people. After you finish visiting with his mother, we may have to re-interview every one again. Keep me posted."

Kevin and Steve pulled their unmarked unit into the yard at the Tucker house where there was a silver Subaru parked beside the mobile home. Kevin noticed that the tag on the car was issued to a fleet and stickers on the rear window indicated that it was a rental.

"Looks like Miss Tucker has company," Kevin said to Steve.

"That tag was issued in Utah," Steve observed. "Looks like maybe the daughter is here."

When Steve and Kevin stepped up on the stoop, the door of the mobile home swung open and a drop dead, gorgeous female dressed in a red halter and blue short shorts stood before them.

"Hi Guys," she said. "My mom saw you through the window. Please come in. I'm Tina and I'm here for a few days helping my mom with things."

When they entered the room Steve noticed that Candice Tucker was sitting in the same place as she was the last time he visited. This time though, she had on a very pretty flowered dress and her hair was pulled back into a bun on the back of her head, and that pistol was stuck between the couch cushions just like before. She spoke to Steve.

"Well young man," she said. "I see you took me up on my invitation to come back."

"In a way I'd say you're right Miss Tucker," Steve replied. "This is my partner Kevin Marcy, and we need to see if you can help us with a problem we have with the investigation of what happened to your son."

"Like I said, we didn't talk a whole lot, but I'll do what I can," Candice lamented.

"When we examined Clintons body," Steve began. "There was a belt buckle missing and he had a small gun holster on his belt but there was no gun in it. I understand that whenever Clinton was off duty, he wore a large belt buckle. Can you describe it for us"? Tina spoke up.

"I can describe it because I gave him that buckle as a birthday present a couple years ago right after he and Mom moved here. It was a white rodeo buckle with gold trim and the Wyoming logo, a cowboy riding a bucking bronco, in the middle. I bought it at a gift shop in the terminal at the Salt Lake City airport."

"That tells me that there was nothing special about it that would distinguish it from any other like it," Kevin said with sigh.

"O yeah," Tina interrupted. "I had his name engraved on the back of it. It said, Clinton J Tucker. He never used his middle name and I'm probably the only one who ever called him Clinton John."

"That might be the best piece of information we've gotten in this case," Kevin said with a smile. "Now, we think Clinton may have had a small handgun that he carried when he was off duty, any knowledge of that"?

"He always had a little gun in a holster that he had in the middle of his back," Miss Tucker advised. "I used to tease him about it. I never saw him without it when he was out of uniform. In his bedroom is a gun chest. Whenever he took his guns off, he'd put them in the chest where he kept some rifles and a couple of shot guns. I know because he was always cleaning them and making sure they were secured in that chest. Tina, why don't you show them the chest. The key is in a bag on the dresser with his personal things that we got from the police department."

When Tina opened the gun locker there were two rifles, a browning 306 and a Remington 30-30; a Winchester pump 12 gage shot gun and a Smith and Weston 357 magnum handgun. On the inside of one of the cabinets doors was a list of all the guns to include serial numbers. There was a 38 caliber Colt Detective Special, with a two-inch barrel listed but not in the cabinet. Steve wrote down the serial number in his pocket notebook. Kevin turned to Tina and thanked her for all the information that had been provided, said good day to Miss tucker on their way out and headed back to the sheriff's department. On the way they discussed the value of the information they had gleaned.

"We need to have someone check that belt buckle that Jess Preston was wearing the other day," Steve said.

"When I get to the office, I'll put a call in and have the jailers over in Evanston check the back of that buckle in Jess's personal property," Kevin replied".

CHAPTER SEVEN

THE **ATMOSPHERE AROUND** the Rock Springs police department was somewhat heavy since the death of officer Tucker. Even though he was mostly a pain in the butt to the supervisory staff, he was one of them; he was a member of the team. Lt. Tobias was the most despondent because Tucker was his man and he had had the closest dealings with him. He kept asking himself, what had he missed? What was there that he should have seen that may have prevented that young man's death?...

Matt Kessler had a difficult time with it too. He had never lost one of his men before. He had been the one to tell Miss Tucker that her son was dead. She didn't say anything for a long time, she didn't cry, she just stared at him. He felt like she wasn't looking at him but through him, at something that only she could see at that moment. When she did speak, he could hardly hear what she said.

"I knew," she had said. "I knew when he didn't come home last night, he wasn't coming. For a long time I've feared that this day would come, but I guess I just wasn't ready."

Matt knew that there would probably be an emotional response to the news, so he had asked Maggie to go with him to deliver the news. After he gave Miss Tucker the news, he went outside and left Maggie with her. Telling that lady that her son was dead was the hardest thing he'd ever done.

"She's a strong woman," Maggie said as they were headed back to the PD. "She'll be alright."

"I can't imagine what it's like to lose your child," Matt commented. "It was devastating for me when I lost my wife a few years back. I

thought my life was over. We didn't have any kids so there was really nothing for me to cling to."

"All this time I've been at the department, I never knew," Maggie said.

"It was way before your time Maggie," Matt began. I had just taken this job when we got the news that she was in stage four cancer. It went fast, within a few months after her diagnosis she was gone. If it weren't for this job I don't know if I could have made it; but that's enough of the past. Now that your divorce has been finalized you must feel that a heavy load is off your shoulders."

"Actually, no," Maggie replied. There was a sadness in her voice. "I invested a little over ten years in that marriage, ten years of my life, and I have nothing to show for it except a heavy heart. I can't help but feel somewhat responsible for the situation that Earnest is in. It's really because of me that he's where he is."

"You didn't make him go stupid," Matt interjected. "He did what he did all on his own. You had no part in his decision."

"I know that Matt," but I still feel badly."

"Hell"!! He tried to kill you Maggie"!! Matt exclaimed.

"Yes, and if it weren't for Kevin at the Sheriff's Office, he would have gotten it done too," Maggie stated...

Kevin made a call to the Evanston facility and requested that they check the buckle in Jess's personal belongings. It wasn't long before his call was returned.

"This is Kevin Marcy," he'd answered the phone.

"Hello there Kevin. This is Sergeant Kravitz in Evanston," came the reply. "I've got that buckle in front of me, what was it you needed"?

"Turn it over sarge and look on the back," Kevin directed. "What do you see"?

"Nothing really, Kevin," Sergeant Kravitz said. "Looks like somebody took a rotary file to it. There may have been a name engraved on it, but it's been filed off."

"Thanks Sergeant Kravitz, that gives me what I needed to know," Kevin said and terminated the call.

Kevin sat for some time thinking about what he had been told about the buckle, then he turned to Steve Lolly who was at his desk across the room. He relayed what he had been told by the Sergeant at Evanston.

"I'm convinced that that's the buckle that belonged to Tucker," Kevin said.

"If your gut is talking to you, maybe you ought to make a trip down there and talk to Jess," Steve advised. The following day Kevin did just that.

When they escorted Jess into the interview room, he was dressed in an orange jump suit, his hair was disheveled, and he hadn't shaved for a couple of days. He appeared to have been awaken from a nap.

"Hey Jess," Kevin greeted him. "I'm Kevin Marcy from the Sweetwater County Sheriff's Office. I need to ask you some questions."

"What about," Jess inquired.

"I'm investigating the death of a police officer and you may be able to help me," Kevin informed him.

"Hell man, I'm in enough trouble I don't know anything about any Killen," Jess shouted out.

"I'd like to ask you a few questions anyway," Kevin said, and he proceeded to advise Jess of his rights. Jess said that he understood what his rights were and agreed to answer Kevin's questions.

"You have a Wyoming Rodeo type buckle in your personal belongings, is it yours"? Kevin asked.

"Yeah," Jess replied. "it's mine."

"Did you buy it new"? Kevin continued to probe.

"No, I didn't buy it new," Jess replied.

"Where'd you get it"? Kevin asked.

"I bought it off a guy," Jess related.

"When did you buy it off a guy"? Kevin wanted to know.

"It's been a while back," Jess said. "Maybe a month or more."

"How did you come to buy that buckle from this guy"? Kevin continued to probe.

"I was at a gas station," Jess said looking at the ceiling remembering the encounter, "This guy comes up and asks me if I wanted to buy a buckle, and he showed it to me. I always wanted one of those, so I said yeh and asked him how much. He said he wanted twenty dollars for it. I gave him a couple of tens and that's how I got the buckle."

"Where was this gas station, Jess"? Kevin asked.

"It was the North Get-N-Go on Elk Street," Jess replied. "I always gas up there."

"Tell me Jess, was there anything engraved on the back of the buckle"? Kevin asked.

"There might have been at one time, but it had been rubbed out," Jess told Kevin.

"What did this guy look like that sold you the buckle"? Kevin wanted all the information he could get on this situation.

"Don't remember a whole lot about him," Jess said. "He had real sharp facial features and his nose looked like it didn't belong on it. He wore a knitted cap and there was bright red hair sticking out the bottom. That's all I remember."

There were three pawn shops in Rock Springs, one in Green River and a shady character in Wamsutter that bought and sold stuff. He did have a firearm dealers license, but he did not possess a brokers permit. There had been no complaints about his dealings, and he dealt mostly with oil field Roughnecks which was a very transit group. Kevin decided that it was time to check and see if anyone had pawned a handgun with a serial number that matched the one, he had jotted down in his pocket pad.

In the last month or so, the Green River Pawn and Loan had only taken in a Smith & Weston AR 15 Rifle, a Browning Pump Shot Gun and a Barretta thirty-Eight Caliber automatic, all belonging to the same customer who needed money to go back to Kansas because his wife was having a baby. The Rock Springs HOCK SHOP had two handguns being held and awaiting retrieval but neither serial number matched.

Kevin stopped in at the ACME Pawn and Loan as he continued his quest for Officer tucker's gun. The owner, Ed Roseburg, was a retired Rock Springs PD officer and his place was frequented by enforcement officers, county court personnel and active-duty uniformed officers. Ed always kept the coffee on and there was always some of his retired buddies, local lawyers or other county officials just hanging out in the shop. Ed had set up a coffee nook of sorts to accommodate them. On this day there were only three people there when Kevin walked in; a uniformed city police officer, who Kevin did not know, Strome Cooper a buddy of Eds and Peter Stricker, the Sweet Water County District Judge.

After greetings all around Kevin took a Styrofoam cup from the stack on the coffee stand, filled it half full of coffee. Ed had placed a large, framed picture of wild horses on the wall above the stand that the pot was on and Kevin couldn't help taking a moment to admire it, then took a seat on a stool that Ed pulled up for him.

"Don't see you around very often Kevin," Ed Commented. "What brings you this way"?

"Working a case," Kevin replied. "Stopped in to see if maybe somebody may have unloaded a piece of evidence with you."

"I hope not," Ed said. "The last time I turned a piece of evidence over to the county I never got re-imbursed".

"I hope not too," spoke up Judge Stricker behind a chuckle. "Don't think I can be a witness in my own court."

"It's a long shot, but I have to eliminate the possibility," Kevin said.

"You working that Tucker case by chance"? Ed asked.

"Yeh," responded Kevin. "why do you ask"?

"Just being nosey," Ed shrugged. "Clinton used to come and stand by while I closed, when he was on duty. I really liked him, but he had problems."

"Care to enlighten me"? Kevin inquired.

"A couple of days before he was killed, he asked me to loan him some money," Ed began. "I'd loaned him a couple of times before, but I just didn't have it to spare this time."

"Care to divulge how much he was trying to borrow"? Kevin asked.

"Hell, the guy's dead now it don't matter," Ed said sorrowfully. "He said he needed a hundred fifty to get his mom some pain meds."

"Did he by chance say where he was going to get the meds"? Kevin pressed.

"No. He didn't say, and I didn't ask. I didn't want to know," Ed stated.

While Ed and Kevin were casually discussing Ed's relationship with Clinton there was the sound of chimes, someone had entered and stepped on the mat in front of the door, activating the chimes. Ed left to care for the customer. Several minutes passed and Kevin took the last sip of his coffee. Over the rim of his cup he could see the reflection of the customer through the glass that was in the framed wild horses. It was one of the people that he had interviewed regarding the death of Officer Tucker.

While the staff at the SO was busy with the Clinton Tucker investigation, Amy and Fred Dreskel found themselves having to provide security for several people at the hospital. One of them was a middle- aged female named Clareice, that had been removed from a bus by the Rock Springs PD. According to the report submitted by the officer that decided she needed help, Clareice had informed everyone on the bus that people at NORAD (North American Aerospace

Command) in Colorado Springs, CO. had placed an electronic device in her vagina so when she was kidnaped by aliens they would be able to monitor goings on when they tried to mate with her. She insisted on showing passengers where the device had been placed and kept removing her clothes after several women tried to keep her dressed. Apparently Clareice had informed the Fort Collins Police Department that she had family in Salt Lake City, Utah. With the help of a local church organization they had purchased a bus ticket and sent her on her way. Amy had managed to contact her family and Clareice was being held until she'd be picked up.

Then there was Richard, a young man in his early twenties, who had tried to hurt himself because he was Gay, and his family had told him he had to leave their home. He was being held because he was a danger to himself and until arrangements could be made for a psychiatric evaluation.

The third detainee was heart wrenching. A female child, estimated to be about four years old, Caucasian with brown curly hair had been abandoned at the truck stop west of Rock Springs. One of the cleaning ladies had observed the child sitting in the TV lounge when she had come on duty early in the morning. The little girl was dressed in a nice jean outfit. When she was still there at noon, she decided to speak with her. When she asked the little girl if her mommy and daddy knew where she was, there was no indication that the child heard her. When she sat beside her, the girl turned to face her. Again the question about her parents was put to her. The girl placed her finger on the cleaning ladies lips, then touched her own and shook her head. She also touched her ears and again shook her head. The lady realized that the child could not talk and worst, couldn't hear. She reported the situation, and the Sheriff's Office was notified.

Because of the unique circumstances, social services officials in Green River decided that they would turn the child over to Child Protective Services that had offices in Cheyenne. Sherrie at the SO decided that the best place for the child would be at the hospital under the watchful eye of CPI people until the officials in Cheyenne could pick her up. Amy had arranged for two beds to be placed in one of the rooms and had already spent two days with the child. The hospital staff saw to it that there was coloring books and crayons available and would take her around to visit with other children that were patients at the hospital.

After the elections were over and Craig Spence would no longer be the sheriff of Sweetwater County, Fred and Amy decided that this would be a good time to cease operations of CPI. Current contracts with the federal government in all seven states were up for renewal and the easiest way out would be to advise procuring agencies now that CPI did not intend to continue providing services and would not be bidding on future contracting opportunities.

The most pressing reason that they wanted to cease operations was Amy's health. The long days supervising staff, handling personnel problems and the sleepless nights manning the detention rooms at the hospital was taking its toll on her all of a sudden. She lacked energy, she began suffering with headaches and experiencing cramps in her extremities. A visit to the family doctor had resulted in a battery of test being performed and the resulting diagnosis was that she had contracted Hepatitis C, a disease generally associated with druggy's and the sharing of needles. The question that she wrestled with was, where did she get it?

Her doctor, in an effort to put Amy's mind at ease, had her think back over her adult life and recall situations in which she could have been exposed to Hep C. She could have contracted it through interactions with people as a police officer, spital, blood or other bodily fluids. Amy related that she had had back surgery early on in her adult life. During the procedure she began to bleed and had to have a transfusion. Her doctor determined that it was before Hep C was discovered and blood was not checked for it before being administered. That's probably where she contracted the disease, and it can take many years before symptoms manifest themselves. Amy was advised that there was no cure and that her liver and other organs would be impacted by the disease.

Amy and Fred were devastated when they first got the news, but Amy pulled herself together and decided that she would like to get the most out of the rest of her life. She told Fred that she would like to go back to the town in New Mexico where she was raised and he agreed, CPI would cease to exist after Sheriff Craig Spence leaves office and that she should prepare to return to New Mexico while he closed out the business. They decided that Amy could fall back on her previous talents and find a house and get them established.

Prior to becoming a police officer, Amy had worked for a real estate company in Las Cruces New Mexico, a small town on the edge of the Chihuahuan Desert and bordering the Rio Grande River. This is where Amy had grown up, attended High School and became a real estate agent. It was in Las Cruces that Amy met her first husband who was associated with governmental defense contracting. Eventually, differences and infidelity issues on his part led to a divorce and Amy, who now had four small children, picked up and moved to Ft. Collins, Colorado where she joined the Larimer County Sheriff's Department.

After graduating from High School, three of her children, a daughter and two sons, moved to Wyoming while a second daughter went off to college on the west coast. It wasn't long before the kids invited their mother to come live with them in Rock Springs, Wyoming. Amy accepted and in the pursuit of employment opportunities, met Fred.

The ACME Pawn and Loan had a log glass counter that ran from the entrance to about three quarters way through the interior. Behind the counter many of the items that were for sale were displayed and Ed Rosenberg kept a filing cabinet with specification document, sales receipts and other stuff. Pawn shops generally have a working relationship with Law enforcement entities and readily share information upon request.

As Kevin was leaving, Ed was still behind the counter, and beckoned to Kevin.

"Did you by chance see the customer that was just in here," Ed Asked.

"Yeah," Kevin responded. "He was one of the people that I interviewed about the Tucker case."

"Well, you might be interested in this," Ed said as he moved a big brown envelop in front of Kevin.

Kevin carefully opened the envelope and removed its contents, a 38 Detective Special, snub nosed handgun.

"The guy wanted one hundred dollars for it, and I wasn't even interested in taking it because I've got too many in inventory now, but when I checked the serial number against my records I decided to offer him fifty and he said okay. I sold that piece six months ago. I sold it to Clinton Tucker."

Kevin took out his pad that he had jotted the serial number from the list on Tuckers cabinet door. The number in his pad matched the number on the gun.

"Could you make me a copy of the sales slip"? Kevin was excited. Pawn brokers will always ask for a government approved ID and record the information before making a sale. The name on the sales slip was Pete Lomas, the number two bartender at the Crystal Pistol.

When Craig arrived at the morning meeting everyone was rather jovial, and everyone greeted him in unison.

"Good morning sheriff."

"Good morning", Craig replied. "I would expect that with all the moving and chaos around here there would be a different atmosphere. Where are we on the move anyway"? Sherrie spoke up.

"Please take all your personal stuff out of your office sheriff, we saved your office till last and today is the day," she said. "This is the

last meeting we will have here. Our next meeting will be in the new building."

"Never thought I'd see it," Craig said. I'll even get to hang around in it for a month or so."

"Yes sir," Sherrie agreed. "I like the new place and you can be proud of what you accomplished."

"We like it too," Steve jumped into the conversation. "We've all got separate entrances to our offices, there are no stairs to climb, and boss, you would not believe the dispatch suite. The equipment in it is first class."

"It was you guys that said what you wanted and I'm just glad that it all worked out. Sherrie, as usual you get to go first."

"Of course we have no one detained here in the old county jail," she began. "We will begin to relocate prisoners that we farmed out to other counties by the end of the week. We do have some detainees at the hospital. We have a young female, who is deaf and dumb. She was abandoned at the west end truck stop. We are just holding her until Child Protective Services can pick her up. That should happen today. Amy, the co-owner of CPI, has been spending a lot of time with her. When she was getting her undressed the first night, Amy found a note that was taped to the inside of her shoe. The girl apparently didn't even know it was there. I have a copy of it I'll read it to you".

"To whom it might concern,
This is Kaylee. We are homeless.
We Can't care for her any longer.
She needs help that we can't give her.
She doesn't speak and can't hear".

"We also have Clarice, a middle-aged female who thinks NORAD has placed a device of some kind in her body where the sun doesn't shine. Her family has been contacted and she'll be picked up, hopefully today. Then there's Richard, a young man that tried to hurt himself and he's to be held until he can be evaluated, and the court will determine what happens to him. That's all that's happening in my world, sheriff."

"I can't imagine the courage it takes to abandon your child in the hope that it will be able to get the help that you can't give. In today's world, under today's laws, if these parents were found, they would pay a high price for the way they tried to help their baby girl. What cha got Steve"?

"Well boss, Kevin and I will be talking about the same thing, the Tucker case. We believe that we've finally gotten a break in the case. Not only have we found the buckle that was missing from officer Tuckers belt, we have also found and have in evidence officer Tuckers off duty weapon and we now have a suspect. I'll let Kevin fill you in."

"Jess Preston bought the buckle off an individual at the North Get-N-Go on Elk street," Kevin began. "He described the male individual to me, and I made note of it. Now this is the crazy part. I stopped in at Ed Rosenberg's place to get a cup of his coffee, and while I'm sitting there this guy comes in and I recognize him as one of the people I talked to from the Pistol. When I was leaving Ed called me over and shows me this gun that the guy had pawned with him. He tells me that he sold the gun to Clinton Tucker. I check the serial number and it matches the serial number that we copied off the sheet on Tuckers gun cabinet. Then it dawns on me, this guy matches the description of the guy that sold the buckle to Jess. I ask Ed for a copy of the pawn slip and the name on it is Peter Lomas, the number two bartender at the Pistol. I intend to have another talk with Mr. Lomas."

"That happened to me some years ago," Craig related. "I was investigating the theft of some office equipment and I was in the pawn shop when the thief brought in one of the items I was looking for. This could be the break you've been looking for Kevin. Let's see what we have here." Craig always brought a pad f paper with him to these meetings and he positioned it directly in front of him, took a pencil and a pen from the breast pocket of his shirt, selected the pencil and placed the pen back in the pocket. He wrote in the upper left-hand corner of the top sheet of paper, Clinton Tucker (Victim-deceased-homicide).

"We know that Officer Tucker was in the pistol for some time the night he died. Whom did he associate with during the time he was there, Steve"?

"He spoke with the bar tender and one of the waitresses," Steve recalled.

Craig placed a note on his pad referencing contacts and asked, "What was the conversations about, do we know"?

"He supposedly wanted the bartender to take a break so that he could get some pain pills and give them to him," Steve replied. "As for the waitress, they just commented about her keeping his seat warm."

"There was phone call made by Clinton and he also met with Lt. Tobias that night," Kevin said.

"DO we know if the bar tender took a break and get the pills for Clinton"? Craig asked.

"No sir, he did not take a break," Steve responded.

"What about Tobias, what was that all about," Craig continued to search for answers.

"There was some dispute about a letter or some disciplinary action that Tobias had taken regarding Tucker, Steve said. "Tucker had asked Tobias to stop by the pistol and discuss it. They met early on during the night at Tobias's car on the street and after the meeting Tucker returned to his seat at the end of the bar."

"Is there any indication that Tobias returned at any time during the night"? Craig asked.

"No sir," Steve answered.

"Can we eliminate Tobias as a suspect"? Craig asked. Both Steve and Kevin agreed that Tobias could be eliminated.

"Kevin," Craig continued. What do we know about the phone call"? who did he make the phone call to"?

"Have no idea, Sheriff," Kevin responded. Craig made notes on the pad and put a question mark beside the one about the phone call.

"Was there any one of the people you two interviewed that was outside the place at anytime that Tucker might have been outside"? Craig asked. "Anyone that may have had time to do Tucker in and maybe go back inside without anyone knowing what had happened"? Steve and Kevin looked at each other and both began looking through their interview reports. Craig realized that Sherrie was still sitting at the table. "Sherrie, I'm sorry. Unless you have something I should know, you can leave. We might be a while."

"I do have something Sheriff. Don't come here tomorrow. We'll be working from the new offices from now on. If you'll make sure all your personal stuff is boxed up, I'll have it taken over this afternoon."

"Will do," Craig answered. "That's great news. See you tomorrow unless something unforeseen happens."

"Here we go"! Kevin exclaimed. "Carla Denton, one of the cocktail waitresses told me that she and Pete took the trash out together, and Clinton went out the back door with them. Pete didn't go back in with her, he stayed and tried to shut the dumpster."

"What about Clinton"? Craig asked.

"She said she had no idea where he went," Kevin said reading from his report of the interview.

"OK," Craig said. "We have Pete the bartender outside: we have Clinton outside; and Clinton ends up dead; his belt buckle and off duty weapon ends up missing ; Jess Preston ends up with the buckle sold to him by a guy whose description matches Pete Lomas and Pete Lomas pawns the gun. We've got some lose ends to tie up. I've got a hunch that the phone call may have been to Jess Preston. Remember, he was on probation for moving drugs and if I recall reading in one of your reports that Pete had told you that Clinton usually got his pills from someone else and he had given him some of his occasionally. We need to talk to him again. Then we need to talk to Pete Lomas again, this time as a suspect. What do you two think"?

"I think Pete's our guy," Kevin concluded.

"I think so too boss," Steve agreed.

"So do I, but I'm thinking way ahead of you. When we try to present this to the county attorney, we need to have an answer to everything. Who did Clinton make that phone call too? The answer could blow everything up in our faces. If in fact Pete is our guy, why did he kill Clinton"? Soon as you guys get set up in your new offices, get on it. I think you got something."

CHAPTER EIGHT

CRAIG ONLY TOOK a few things to the new office. He wasn't going to be there long so he wouldn't need much. There was a private entrance to the sheriff's office, and it opened into a small dressing room. There was a large mirror over a countertop, a chair with a matching couch, and off to one side of the room was a small shower stall with an accompanying sink and medicine cabinet. *What a deal*, Craig thought.

An inner door opened into an office suite. It was huge and it was furnished like a hotel suite. A large mahogany desk was situated in the middle of the outside wall and a beautiful executive chair just waited to be tested. As he sat at the desk Craig was impressed with the full-length glass top on the desk and there were drawers on both pedestals, not just one side like his old desk. Someone had hung all of the pictures, awards and certificates from the old office on the walls and had set up the display cases at the far end of the room.

There were two other inner doors and Craig found the one in the center of the inner wall opened into a waiting room where his administrative assistant now had a well designed and roomy cubicle arrangement, and she was there.

"Good morning Heather," Craig greeted her. "How do you like it"? He was referring to her new workstation.

"This is downtown Sheriff," Heather responded. "Its going to be a pleasure to come to work."

"I get it," Craig said as he walked back into his office. When he opened the other door, he found himself in the dispatch area. There was electronic consoles all along the walls of a smoked glass enclosure,

and there were lights everywhere, some blinking but most were static. He eased back into his office so as not to disrupt the operation. Just as he closed the door, Sherrie entered from the outer office.

"Well Sheriff," She inquired. "How do you like it"?

"As Heather would say, this is downtown," Craig responded.

"If you got time, come I'll give you a tour of the complex," Sherrie offered.

"Got all day," Craig told her. "Lead on."

Steve and Kevin found their offices spacious also and what was really neat was a commons area where people could wait comfortably until it was their turn to be interviewed. They lounged in the stuffed chairs while discussing the case at hand.

"I've gone over the events and evidence several times," Kevin was saying. "I believe we have enough to Pick him up."

"If we go and place him under arrest, he's gonna clam up tighter than a vice", Steve surmised. "Somehow, we need to approach this so that he'll want to talk. We need to know why and how he did it."

"What you got in mind", Kevin wanted to know.

"First, I think we ought to talk to Jess Preston and see if Clinton Tucker called him that night and why," Steve said. "Jess is here now so let me go talk to him and then I'll get back with you."

Later in the day Steve came into Kevin's office. He had visited with Jess Preston.

"Clinton Tucker did call Jess that night," Steve began. "Before Jess was busted for moving drugs, he had been Clintons supplier. Jess says that Clinton knew that he was on probation, but Clinton told him that he was desperate. Jess says that Clinton told him that his Mom was out of pain pills and he needed to have some that night. Jess told him that he wasn't doing that stuff anymore and that he didn't have what he needed. He says Clinton slammed the receiver down and that's the last time he spoke with him."

Kevin took a folder out of the middle drawer of his desk and began to run his finger back and forth over the pages, then he removed a page and handed it to Steve.

"This is a copy of my interview with Pete," Kevin said. "He told me that sometimes he would give Clinton some pills to hold him over until he could get some from some other source."

"You think Clinton was trying to hit Pete up for some pills," Steve asked.

"Could be," Kevin said. "Something went wrong. When did he have time to do it"? Kevin thought for a moment. "Ah yes. When Pete and the bar maid took the trash out, Clinton went out with em, but Pete didn't go back in with the bar maid and Pete said he saw Clinton go toward a car and that was the last time he saw him. He lied."

"looks like it," Steve agreed. "I've got an idea. Let's have a deputy pick him up. That in itself will make him nervous. We'll tell him we need to tie up some loose ends and we need to go over some of the stuff he told us. We'll set him in one of the interview rooms. When the doors to those rooms close, they lock, and we have to use a remote to open them. We can watch him through the two-way glass in the wall of the room. We'll let him stew in there a few minutes, then I'll go in with the Buckle and the gun and put them on the table. You knock on the door and tell me I have a phone call and I'll come out, leaving the buckle and the gun on the table, and we can watch how he reacts. He'll tell us a lot by his realization that we have both items. When we think he's had enough, we'll just go in and ask him if there is anything he'd like to tell us."

"Let's run this by the boss first," Steve said. "The last thing we want is to screw this up."

Craig listened very attentively to his two investigators and at Craigs insistence they all three presented "What If" scenarios in effort to plug any holes in the case. Finally Craig was ready to make a decision.

"I don't like the idea of tricking this guy into coming down here," Craig began. "I can just see some smart lawyer throwing it back in our faces. I think you have enough to get a warrant for his arrest. There is no way he can explain his way out of having those missing items in his position other than him being at the scene. Get a warrant, arrest him and then let him stew."

As a matter of professional courtesy, while Steve and Kevin worked on getting the warrant, Craig drove over to the Rock Springs police department to brief Matt Kessler. As he entered the office he was greeted by a radiant Maggie.

"Well, Sheriff Spence," she said as she came from behind her desk. "It's so nice to see you," she said as she gave Craig a big hug and he took off his cowboy hat and put it on top of her head.

"it's good to see you too doll," he said with a big smile. "Is your boss in"? Maggie checked the phone on her desk.

"He's on the phone right now but I don't think he'll be long," she advised. "Have a seat and we can visit a bit."

"I don't think I've seen you since your divorce has been final," Craig began. "How does it fell to be a free woman"?

"At first it was a little sorrowful and scary," she replied. "But as time has gone on, I've gotten over the shock and realize that it was the right thing to do. I've begun to go on with my life."

"I'm going to be nosey," Craig said. "Does going on with your life include Kevin"?

"Kevin and I are really good friends," Maggie said. "He understands that I'm not ready to jump into a serious relationship, but I like having him around," she said smiling. "Oh, the Chief is off the phone." She pushed a button on the phone. "Sheriff Spence to see you." The door to Matts office opened and Matt rushed out with his hand extended and he and Craig shook hands.

"Good to see you Craig," Matt said. "Been meaning to call you, haven't heard anything about your investigation."

"That's why I'm here, Matt-and I'm sorry for not coming in sooner," Craig apologized as they walked into Matts office.

Craig meticulously walked Matt through the investigation conducted by his people, from start to finish, and he advised Matt that there was a suspect and that there was a warrant being sought.

"We believe we've got a pretty solid case against one of the people that works at the Pistol," Craig was saying as Maggie walked in with two cups of coffee. She sat a cup in front of each man and exited as quickly as she had come in.

"When do you plan to make the arrest," Matt asked.

"Steve and Kevin are after the Warrant now," Craig advised. "As soon as it is secured, they'll bring him in. Would you like to set in on the interrogation"?

"Yeah", Matt said. "In fact, I'd like to be with you when you make the arrest. Politically I think it will serve us both well to proceed that way. I'd like to hear what the person has to say, then I can thoroughly brief my people."

"Okay, I'll give you a buzz when we're ready," Craig said as he walked toward the office door and out into the outer office. He picked up his hat off the desk where Maggie had put it, said his goodbyes and was gone.

Craig and his staff along with Matt and Pappy decided that the best place to take Pete in custody would be the Crystal Pistol, before it opens, while preparations are being made by the bartenders, stocking and getting ready for opening. The plan was to make sure that Pete would be behind the bar when things went down, that way the possibility of him running is minimized and if he did try to, the five of them would be able to take him down. Paul, the owner of the Pistol was advised of the plan and was available to open the front door when the team arrived.

When the team entered the Pistol, sure enough, Pete was behind the bar removing cans of beer from boxes and placing them in coolers. Members of the team-Kevin, Steve, Craig, and Pappy Masters positioned themselves strategically around the bar in case things went south. Matt got Pete's attention.

"Pete Lomas," Matt called out. Pete stood up and responded.

"Yes, I'm Pete Lomas, what can I do for you"? The men standing around the room, all in uniforms of the Sheriffs Department and Rock Springs PD caused his heart to beat so loud he could hear it in his ears. He knew why they were there.

"Pete Lomas," Matt called out. "I'm placing you under arrest for the murder of Officer Clinton Tucker." Matt continued to advice Pete

of his rights to remain silent and his right to have an attorney present during any questioning. Pete immediately requested an attorney.

It was decided that Pete would be booked into the County Detention facility rather than at the Rock Springs Police Department Jail to avoid any reprisals from RSPD personnel. An attorney from the Public Defenders office was requested to meet with Pete prior to any questioning.

The door to the interrogation room opened and a young blond female, carrying a brief case entered.

"You Mr. Pete Lomas," She asked, and he responded that he was. "I'm Melody Papas and I'm from the Public Defenders Office. I believe you requested the assistance of an attorney. I need to get some basic information from you and then you tell me why you're in here"....

Pete was arranging trash bags in the dumpster so that he could close the lid when Tucker came up beside him.

"Hey man," Tucker had said. "My regular guy is out of business and I really need those pills."

"You haven't paid me for the ones I gave you a couple of weeks ago," was Pete's reply. "I have to buy more, so when you pay me, I'll be able to help you." At that time tucker had grabbed Pete's shoulder and spun him around. Regaining his balance Pete began walking hurriedly toward the back door of the Pistol. Tucker followed. Just before Pete reached the door Tucker again grabbed him.

"You Son of a Bitch," Tucker said menacingly. "You know what I need those pills for," and he again shoved Pete. This time Pete lost his balance and fell down beside the building. Tucker was right after him, grabbing Pete by the front of his jacket, all the while shouting in his face about what a shit ass he was and shaking him. Pete reached out, felt the rocked flower bed and tried to pull himself up; the rock came off in his hand; he swung it at Tucker and struck him in the face. Tucker let go of him and Pete pulled himself up and ran. For reasons unknown to him, he had run back to the dumpster. He also realized that he still had the rock in his hand. He put the rock in the dumpster and put the lid down. When he went to the back door of the Pistol, he saw Tucker, on all fours, making groaning noises. That's when the

thought came to him about the buckle, he could sell it and get some of the money that Tucker owed him.

He ran over and pushed Tucker over, undid his belt and took the buckle. He then saw the gun that was in a holster attached to the belt. He decided to take it because it would sell for a bunch more. Tucker was still breathing and moaning when he left…

After about an hour Melody had all the information she needed and proceeded to give Pete instructions.

"You will probably go before a judge tomorrow and be arraigned. I'll be there with you. Because you're being charged with murder the chances that I can get a bond set for you is questionable, but I'll try. During the arraignment I'll do all of the talking. The only time I want you to speak is when you are asked how you intend to plea, and I want you to say, not guilty. Do you understand"?

"Yeah, but you look awful young for me to be putting my life in your hands," Pete responded.

"What you see is what you've got," Melody said-somewhat offended. "There is little doubt that the victim in this case probably died as a result of your actions. It is also evident that you acted in self-defense, and that's where we're headed. I want you to co-operate in every way with the police except when it comes to this case. If they want information, they talk to me, Understood?

"Yep," Pete replied, feeling somewhat more comfortable with the take charge attitude of this young lady. Melody went out to get Craig, Matt and Kevin who were waiting patiently for her to finish her visit with Pete.

The room was a little crowded, but they managed to fit everyone. Matt and Craig stood behind Kevin on one side of the table while Melody sat with Pete on the other side. Melody spoke first.

"I've instructed my client to cooperate as much as he can with your investigation, and I've also instructed him to only answer questions regarding this case when I am present. If you wish to ask Mr. Lomas questions pertaining to his possible involvement of Mr. Tucker's demise, we'll try to provide you answers." Kevin Began the conversation.

"Before we get into the questions, be advised that this interview is being recorded." Getting no objections Kevin began. "It has been brought to our attention that a Belt buckle, that has been identified as one belonging to Officer Tucker was sold by an individual meeting your description. Did you ever sell a buckle to anyone"? Pete looked over at Melody and she nodded her head indicating that he should answer the question.

"yes," Pete replied.

"Would you describe the buckle you sold," Kevin asked. "Also how much you sold it for"?

"It was a large rodeo type buckle," Pete began his description of the Buckle. "It was white with gold trim, with the Wyoming Cowboy on a bucking horse in the middle."

"Was there any markings on the buckle that might Identify its owner and how did you come to have the buckle in your possession"? Kevin pursued his line of questioning.

"Don't answer that," Melody spoke up.

"Have you done business with any pawn shops in town recently"? The question caught Pete by surprise, and he hesitated to answer. Melody caught the hesitation and asked if she could be alone with her client. Kevin picked up his pad and led the rest of the observers out of the room.

"Ok, what haven't you told me"? Melody asked.

"I told you I had taken the gun off Tuckers belt," Pete reminded her. "I forgot to tell you I had Pawned it."

"What else did you forget to tell me"? Melody asked-visibly disturbed.

"I've told you everything else," Pete said. "I just forgot to tell you I pawned the gun."

"I should have guessed that you had done something to get the money out of it," Melody told him. "They've got that gun, and they know you pawned it. This is not good. I don't know if I can get them to move on to another question. We'll just see how it goes. She stood and

signaled the others to come in. After everyone was in place, Melody addressed the question.

"As to whether Mr. Lomas has been to a pawn shop recently is irrelevant unless you can tie any visits he may have made to the case at hand," Melody sparred.

"I assure you the answer to the question will be relevant," Kevin countered.

"I advise my client not to answer the question," Melody responded.

Kevin asked to be excused for a minute. He went to his office and returned with a large brown envelope. From it he took an item wrapped in plastic. It was a snub-nosed revolver.

"This weapon was Officer Tuckers off duty gun," Kevin began. "He always had it with him when he was not in uniform. When his body was found, the holster for it was still on his belt, but the gun was missing. Have you ever seen this gun before Pete"?

"Don't answer that," Melody advised.

"The serial number on this gun matches the records of one purchased by Officer Tucker at the pawn shop owned by Mr. Ed Rosenberg in Rock Springs," Kevin continued. "There is a witness that saw you enter the pawn shop, and we have records of the transaction. Now I ask you again, have you ever seen this gun before"?

"If you have a witness and records there is no need for my client to answer the question," Melody said.

"Melody," Kevin began. "I know you are good lawyer and I respect your efforts to protect your client, but I know that your client killed Officer Tucker and I can prove it. What I don't know is what the circumstances were, why he killed him or what led up to Tucker ending up dead".

"From what my client tells me it sounds to me like self-defense," Melody advised.

"Then why don't we cut out the games and let Pete here tell me what happened," Kevin pleaded. Melody thought for a moment, then leaned over to Pete, placed her hand at Pete's ear in a manner that prevented

Kevin from hearing as she whispered something to him. Pete nodded affirmatively and Melody made a statement.

"I'm going to allow my client to tell his story, but I want you to understand that by telling his story he is not confessing to murdering officer Tucker. Though actions taken by my client may have contributed to officer Tucker dying, my client is not confessing to murder. Does everyone understand that"? Kevin turned in his chair so he could see Craig and Matt behind him, each nodded indicating that they understood. Kevin conveyed the understanding.

"We understand," Kevin responded. Our report to the County Attorney will reflect your statement on behalf of your client, but I have a better idea." Kevin opened a small drawer in the table and removed a form, then he continued. "This is a form used for written statements. Why don't we let Pete write out his statement"?

Melody agreed and Kevin collected his evidence, he and the other observers left the room. The writing pad that Kevin used was left in case they needed additional paper.

The interview lasted several hours and at the end Pete was advised that the report would be submitted to the County Attorney where the decision as to charges would be made. His attorney advised him that she would be at his side all through the arraignment and that she would request a bond hearing after that.

"I have no idea how quickly things will move forward," Melody told Pete. "the time you may be incarcerated could be extensive. Is their anyone you want contacted"?

"I have a girl friend who has no idea where I am. I'd like for her to be contacted and the situation I'm in explained," Pete requested.

"Craig and Matt had Kevin to make copies of Pete's statement and they each read and commented to one another about the way things appeared to have gone down.

"Sounds like Officer Tucker got desperate and made a bad decision," Matt surmised. "I wish I had known about his situation, maybe-just maybe I might have been able to get him some help."

"You know Matt," Craig started, leaning back in his chair and pushing his hat to the back of his head. Things happen to teach us lessons. For some reason officer Tucker hadn't been comfortable with asking you or his supervisors for help. Why did he leave his last job, do you know? Do we ever give our guys a chance to sit with us, just kick back and let them unload about things that bothers them, either about the job or their personal lives? That young officer was taking care of his mother the best way he thought he could. We may not agree with the method he took, it got him killed, but it shows that we need to get closer to our people. Get to know them better, their families, what their ambitions are, their problems."

The investigation of Clinton Tuckers murder and moving to the new location had taken up much of Kevins time. Being the type that puts his all into his work there was little time afforded his social life.

In spite of the realization that fraternizing with subordinates is not a good thing, Matt Kessler had on several occasions dinned out with Maggie. To his surprise being with her allowed him to release the pressures that being chief of the department caused. The time, just spent over a meal, was so relaxing-an experience he hadn't had since his wife had passed-and for Maggie, it was a pleasant change from eating crackers and cheese alone in her apartment. Maggie had agreed to the occasional outings only if they were kept as tension relievers and considered as their "Happy Hour". Most businesspeople and many of their associates went to the pistol or to a local hotel bar after work where they held "Happy Hour".

Matt also found the happy hours with Maggie beneficial because it was an opportunity to pick her brain. She knew everything that was going on in the department and she never hesitated to tell him the good, the hilarious and what was potentially going to get him in trouble with the city fathers.

CHAPTER NINE

FOR THE LAST few weeks of Craigs time as sheriff he spent ensuring that there was a smooth transfer. Harry accompanied Craig to all meetings, including commissioner meetings, budget meetings, meetings with the HR people and several meetings with Sarah, the County Attorney.

Harry was also present when Craig met with Fred and Amy from CPI. It would be their last meeting since the affiliation would end at the end of Craigs term. Amy spoke first.

"Saying goodbye is always hard for me but sheriff I want you to know that this one is especially tough," and tears began to weld up in her eyes.

"You guys have been like family to me," Craig said as he took Amy's hand in his. "You can also be proud of yourselves because you proved to the Law enforcement people in this state that your security people aren't a bunch of "Cop wannabe's" but a well organized and professional firm. You guys really saved my bacon all these years and I'll be forever grateful."

"I am very proud of what our people did, but it was more than that that made for a successful partnership sheriff," Fred said. "It was your willingness to think outside the box. It was your inclusion of us in your training sessions and conferences that made us better partners. No matter where I go or what I may do in the future, I'll always tell the story about your people, and the law man we worked with in Wyoming, Craig Spence, sheriff of Sweetwater County."

While Craig and his people were busy moving into the new county sheriff's offices, Martha-with the help of Katie, who had taken a few days off from her job-was busy packing and taking stuff to the local Goodwill facility. The moving company that had been selected were busy loading furniture and the large boxes. The company had sent several women over to help with the packing so it was expected that they would clear out the house and move into the apartment at the retirement complex by the end of the day.

"Mom"? Katie inquired as she taped a box of clothing. "Did you ever realize that you and Dad had so much stuff"?

"We have lived in this house for nigh twenty years my dear," Martha responded. "Its amazing how much we've accumulated over the years. Moving into an apartment is forcing us to downsize and Goodwill Industries is the beneficiary."

"It's great that Dad is okay with moving into a retirement place," Katie commented.

"I have to admit that I was a little surprised," Martha said. "I knew he was okay with moving into an apartment because we had discussed it. I think you might have been responsible for his acceptance of the idea."

"How come Mom," Katie wondered.

"You were the one who suggested that we go look at some of those places," Martha reminded. "The more we saw of them I think the more he became comfortable with the idea. This place being built right here in Green River certainly helped."

The last pieces of furniture and all the boxes had been loaded on the truck and were headed across town to the Senior Manor of Green River, a three-story complex that featured one, two-and three-bedroom apartments. The floor plans of each were different and Martha had requested one of the small one-bedroom units. The movers placed the furniture where she wanted it, so she and Katie only had to unpack the boxes and put things away.

Craig spent this day visiting the offices of all the people he had worked so closely with over the years. Most had been in charge of the same departments since day one and saying goodbye was not easy for any of them. Craig saved Sarah, the County Attorney for last. When he entered her outer offices, Nancy, the receptionist turned in her chair, away from what ever she was doing, and greeted him.

"Hey Sheriff," she said. "Haven't seen you for a while. Guess you've been busy moving into your new digs, huh"?

"Hi Doll," he responded. "You missed me huh? Guess you're gonna have to get used to me not barging in on you, just stopped by to say goodbye."

'That's right," Nancy said in a low voice, almost a sigh. "You're retiring, aren't you? Dang Sheriff just never thought of you riding off into the sunset. Always thought of you as a fixture in this county."

"Even fixtures get put away eventually doll." The conversation was interrupted by Sarah opening her office door.

"I thought that was you out here," she said referring to Craig. "How does it feel to have the load of the Department off your shoulders"?

"You know Sarah," Craig began. "I never really felt like it was a load. I guess I was mostly always trying to help somebody or looking out for my staff or something other than the demands of the office. Also I had a great staff who knew their jobs and were good at what they did."

"Well, that's well said," Sarah responded. "I'm honored that you came by to see me before you left. What will you do now"?

"Martha has already moved us to that new Senior Living place down by the river and tonight will be my first night to sleep there. I wanted to let you know that of all the county attorneys I've worked with over the years, I've enjoyed working with you the best."

"Thank you, Craig, but I've got a surprise for you," Sarah said. "I'm the one who benefited from the relationship. I did pretty well through Law school, and I started out in this job thinking that I had a handle on applying the law. You taught me otherwise. You taught me that there's the law and then there is the application of the law, and its not always black and white statutes that gets you justice. I'll always be grateful to you Craig, but I need you to do me one last favor."

"I turned in my badge Sarah, I no longer can render services," Craig tried to beg off.

"This has nothing to do with official business," she said. "I've been asked to be the featured speaker at the Police Academy Graduation next week or to recommend someone if I can't make it."

"Oh no"!! Craig exclaimed throwing up both hands. "I'm no public speaker and anyway, they'd boo me out of there."

"Craig," Sarah said pursing her bottom lip fending hurt. "Please, this would really put an exclamation point on that stellar career of yours, and it would really help me stay in good stead with the state boys, please say yes."

"Dog Gone it, Nancy," Craig begged. "Why don't you help me"?

"Not me Sheriff," Nancy begged off. "I just work here."

"Nancy," Sarah called out. "You have a copy of that letter requesting me to speak"? With her head bowed and her face hidden by her right hand, Nancy passed the letter to Sarah with her left. Sarah pushed the letter at Craig.

"You'd better be glad I like you," Craig said as he gathered Sarah up in a big bear hug."

"Thank you, thank you, thank you, Craig," Sarah said trying to catch her breath.

Leaving the familiar surroundings and people he had served with and around, saying goodbye had made for a grueling day for Craig. He had nixed any going away parties and such so it was over, and as he drove the family car, a 1977 Chrysler, toward his new home he thought; *a new home, a new life, an old car and an old wife, What the hell, I can do this.*

When he parked the car in the parking lot, in a spot with his apartment number painted on it, 210 was the number, he sat for a moment and looked at the front of the building. Italic letters across the front above the canopied entrance read *THE SENIOR MANOR of Green River.* He then noticed Martha standing under the canopy waiting for him.

"Welcome home Mr. Spence," she greeted him as he approached. Taking his arm she said, "May I escort you to our new home"?

"By all means Mrs. Spence," he responded. Arm in arm they walked through a spacious lobby, passed a large dining area and a dimly lighted bar on one side and offices on the other, to a large elevator at the far end of the lobby where Martha pushed the button with a large number two on it.

When they exited the elevator Craig was looking at the door of apartment 210.

"What a deal," he said. He stood for a moment and took in the spacious hallway with large framed painted scenes all along both sides. Martha handed Craig a set of keys and explained what they were for.

"These are keys to the apartment, the outside entrance which is locked at night at ten PM and our mailbox. The key to our apartment also opens the doors to the pool and the exercise room."

Craig used a key to open the apartment door and walked into the living area. It was larger than the space at the old house and Katie was lounging in one of the comfortable chairs that had been brought over from the old place.

"Welcome home Dad," she said as she came over to give him a hug. "What thinks thou"? Without responding Craig walked toward a large bay window across the room. He could see the town and the river running through it. Across the river he could see Monument Rock, a massive rock formation that changed colors when the sun started its downward plunge each day.

"I had no idea it would be this nice," Craig said in a low voice. "I was prepared to do what ever it took, but this is gonna be easy. I like what I see and it's gonna be easy to get used to."

"Wait until you see the bedroom," Martha said as she led him.

The feature that Martha was happy about was that there in the bedroom was also a large window but different. The window looking out over the city and river was a half-moon with a built-in window seat. That portion of the apartment stuck out away from the main building so that looking out the window on the other side of the room was the desert and the rocky bluffs to the west of town over which the sun set every day, and you could see the traffic on the highway leading out of town to the south.

"Ya did good doll," Craig said complimenting Martha on her choices. He sat on the bed with Martha beside him taking in the view. Katie watched as they seemed to be viewing their new life together. Then Martha spoke.

"It's going to be so nice not to be concerned about getting you off to work in the mornings and then worry about what you are getting involved in on the job. I'm really looking forward to that."

"Oh, I did commit to doing one more thing even though I put my badge away," Craig confessed.

"Craig Spence, you didn't"!! Martha exclaimed getting off the bed and stomping her foot.

"I promised Sarah, Craig began. "you know, the County Attorney. I promised her that I would be the featured speaker at the graduation ceremony for the Police Academy next week." Martha sat back down on the bed.

"Craig, I think that would be a wonderful ending to your career," she said approvingly.

"Martha, you know I'm not good at that type of public speaking," Craig lamented.

"You know how to talk to young people," Martha said as she took his hand. "You'll do just fine, husband of mine, but if you make any more commitments, I'll skin ya."

Craigs first experience with his fellow residence occurred in the dining room, a spacious and elegant space, with chandeliers hanging from the ceiling, large windows that afforded a view of the river and rock formations. As he looked around the room, tables were beautifully set with glasses, plates and silverware, and most had people seated at

them. As he gazed over the room, he was struck by the bobbing heads, multiple shades of grey, visiting with their tablemates. Then he noticed that some of those people were looking at him.

One of the Manors management team saw Martha and Craig standing, looking as if they needed help and approached them.

"My name is Shelley, I'm the Dining Room Hostess," She said. "I believe you are new with us, Welcome. If you are wondering why some of our residence are looking at you, it could be your hat," Shelley said with a giggle. As usual Craig had without thinking put on his cowboy hat as he usually did when he went out.

"We don't wear our hats in the dining room," Shelley advised, "Here, let me have it and I'll put it on the coat rack over by the office door. You can pick it up on your way out." Craig, with apologies, turned over his hat and after placing it on the rack Shelley led them to a table where a couple was already seated and proceeded to introduce them.

"Mertel, Paul, this is a new couple joining our family."

"I'm Martha and this is my husband Craig," Martha said hurriedly, realizing the Hostess didn't know their names. After the hand shaking and the glad to meet you greetings, Martha and Craig seated themselves.

Mertel was a rather attractive woman. It was apparent that she had aged well. She had a full head of heavy salt and pepper hair which she allowed to curl up on top of her head and the sides above her ears and back was trimmed. Her face was somewhat leathery in appearance but not wrinkled, and her eyes were a pale green. Though her hair was salt and pepper, the eyebrows and lashes were jet black. She had big shoulders and her hands were large with thick fingers and the nails were impeccable.

Paul's hair was thinning, and he tried to cover the bald spot in the middle of his head by combing his hair sideways over the top. It was pure white, there wasn't a speck of grey anywhere. His eyes were dark, almost black and the white lashes and brows served to highlight their darkness. He had a thin mustache, and a well-trimmed beard, both as white as snow. Paul was of average height, maybe five-eleven or so, medium build and Martha noticed when she shook his hand that they were very soft. *Office type* she thought. Martha was the first to strike up a conversation.

"Where are you folks from"? She asked Mertel.

"Kalispell, Kalispell Montana," Mertel answered.

"what brought you down here"? Martha probed.

"I was born and raised in Casper and I always said that when I retired I was going to move to Green River," Mertel replied and Craig picked up the conversation with Paul.

"What did you do before coming here Paul"?

"I retired from the Flathead County Public Defender's Office," Paul said. "I spent twenty-three years at it and then Mertel retired from the state Conservation Service, so I retired too."

"You're kidding aren't you"? Craig asked. "About the name of the county I mean"?

"No, that's really the name of the county," Paul answered through a fit of boisterous laughter. "And you Craig, what was your profession before you retired"?

"I spent twenty years as the Sheriff of Sweetwater County," Craig replied and they both burst into laughter.

"And you thought Flathead was funny," Paul chided Craig and they both had a good laugh.

This meeting was the beginning of a close friendship and they frequently visited together at meals, especially the evening meals.

CHAPTER TEN

CRAIG LEFT EARLY in the morning to make the drive to Douglas, Wyoming. That's where the Wyoming Law Enforcement Academy was located. It would be a four hour and fourteen-minute drive. He had tried to entice Martha to ride along for company, but she had declined, electing to take advantage of his absence to get some visiting done with old friends that she had long neglected.

When he arrived he was met by the Academy Director who was waiting and was gracious enough to invite Craig to his office where he had a coffee nook and his own private toilet room, both of which Craig was anxious to take advantage of.

With coffee in hand the two men took the opportunity to get to know a little about one another. Carl Christensen, the Director, was a member of the Wyoming Highway Patrol but was assigned at the Academy. He had been the Director for three years. Craig advised the Director that he and his staff had received their certifications several years prior to his arrival at the Academy.

"Miss Cousins tells me that you have been the Sheriff of Sweetwater County for many years," Carl began.

"Twenty years to be exact," Craig responded. "It's been a hell of a ride."

"I've been with the Patrol for fifteen years, but I don't believe I've ever known anyone that has survived as a sheriff that long," Carl said with a chuckle. "What's your secret"?

"No secret," Craig revealed. "I guess nobody else wanted the job."

"I'll be looking forward to reading the contents of your presentation today," Carl stated. "I'll bet there are some interesting war stories that you'll be telling." Craig pushed his hat to the back of his head, took a sip of coffee and looking at Carl over his cup responded.

"Sorry to disappoint you on both counts Mr. Christensen. First, I have no written remarks, and second, I'll be telling no war stories." There was a moment of uncomfortable silence for Carl. Then Craig continued. "Here at the Academy you provide your students the basics to be a law enforcement officer: Constitutional Law, Search and Seizure requirements and techniques; Laws of Arrest-lots of war stories are related as examples of how to and how not to; Fire Arms training, custody and control-How to hand cuff and what you can and can't do with a hand cuffed person; Emergency Vehicle Operations, how to search a building; Traffic Stops-lots of war stories here, and they are appropriate for training purposes, and then lots of time is spent teaching investigation techniques." Craig stopped a moment and then directed Carl's attention out a window to a patrol car parked in the lot. "On the fender of that patrol car is written what Law enforcement is all about. It Says, "To Protect and Serve. Today I'm going to try and convey how to do that. You here at the Academy teach what I see as the "Hard" Stuff. Today, I'm going to talk about the "Soft" stuff. The stuff that will make an officer successful."

The classroom, though not a large space, had a theater design. Each row of seats were elevated above the row in front of them. The front of the room was a stage and Craig was impressed when Carl and he entered the room Carl pressed a button on the wall and a podium rose from the floor in the center of the stage. Carl walked to the podium and with a button on the side adjusted it to his height.

While Carl addressed the group assembled, Craig observed the audience, he noticed that there was a desk like top in front of each row of seats that ran the length of the row and name tags were in front of each attendee. Craig made a quick count and estimated thirty-five people, and each was in a different uniform, so Craig surmised that there was thirty-five different law enforcement agencies represented. He noticed that there were five women among them.

"Today we are honored to have a man who has become a legend in the area of law enforcement in the state of Wyoming," Carl was saying. "This gentleman grew up on a ranch, did a stint in the United States Navy, and has just recently retired after twenty years as the sheriff of Sweetwater County, Wyoming. In that sheriffs are elected every four years, survival for twenty years in such a political job is unheard of. Ladies and gentlemen, Sheriff Craig Spence."

Craig stepped forward, cowboy hat still in place on his head. There was polite applause. Being shorter than Carl, he remembered the button on the podium and adjusted it and greeted the assemblage.

"Hi ya, hi ya", he said. Not in unison but a resounding Hi ya, hi ya was returned by the audience. Craig removed his hat and laid it onthe podium.

"Eight years ago, I sat where you are," He began. "The state required that all law enforcement people be certified or find another line of work. Never did I think I'd be here today to give a graduating class a sendoff to keep the peace all over the state. I'm honored. From all the different uniforms, I can assume all of you have been exposed to some semblance of the job that you're now certified to do. Now you're ready to strap on that gun, shine up your badge, hit the streets and enforce the law," Craig paused to see if his words had caused any change in the groups attention level. Then he continued.

"By attending this academy you've picked up the saddle and blanket you'll need to ride this bronco, the tools of the trade sort to speak. You pick up the bridle and the reins for a successfully ride when you get out in the community. In other words, this academy does not a peace officer make." He paused again, hoping he'd hit a nerve.

"A little over twenty years ago, someone convinced me to run for sheriff of Sweetwater County. The county was full of railroad workers and coal miners, ranch hands and sheep herders. I was just out of the Navy where I was a championship boxer, so I was pretty cocky. I won the election, spent pretty close to a month riding herd on the outgoing sheriff and on December thirty-first, he gifted me a book of Wyoming Statutes, tipped his hat, and wished me luck."

There was some snickering at his description of his beginnings in keeping the peace and Craig used the brief break to take a sip of water from a glass that Carl had placed on the podium.

"Trial and error is not the best way to succeed at this job, but by the end of my first year in office I had learned some very valuable lessons. The first lesson I learned is stenciled on the rear quarter panel of most of your patrol cars. "To Protect and Serve." It does not say – Judge, Jury and Executioner." Craig noticed that there was a confused look on some of the faces staring down at him. He was sure that they were wondering where he was going with his comments, so he began again to explain in a way only he could.

"I found that to be a lawman in this state, you need to read from two books. One is a hard back and the other has a soft cover. The hard back contains all the state statutes from spiting on the sidewalk to first degree murder and some other sundry offenses; guidelines that allow you to act and represent the state and enforce its laws, and if they are violated a peace officer can cart the violator off to jail or write a citation. Let's take a couple examples; Public Drunkenness, there is a law against that. You can be arrested and put in jail. Disorderly Conduct, there's a law against that, and the offender can be arrested and hauled off to the hoosegow. Driving under the influence, Theft, Burglary, Assault and Murder. A person can be arrested in each of these cases, the only difference is how the peace officer handles them and the amount of time violators may cool their heels in a crossbar hotel, if convicted, or the amount of their hard-earned cash that they may have to share with the county. The most important lessons I learned came from the imaginary book with the soft cover. This book had five chapters: **Respect** was the title of the first chapter. Everyone, no matter who or what they are: The cow poke that punches cows for a living; the elected official accused of corruption; the husband of the housewife that's being abused; the town drunk, that kid walking down the road with his pants hanging down below his buttocks, with so many trinkets in his nose and ears he looks like somebody hit him in the face with a fishing tackle box-and yes, a convicted felon whom you may have an occasion to come across, deserves the same respect. Through the years, respect I showed the people of Sweetwater County, and them that passed through, brought respect for me and the people who worked for

me. Respect earned us the bridle and reins we needed to control that horse called Peacekeeper." When Craig paused this time he noticed a greater level of attentiveness. They were listening.

"The second chapter of that book with the soft cover," Craig went on. "That chapter was called **Patience**. I've had young officers, when sent on a call, act like they're gonna be late for a hot date. No consideration of the situation or the people involved at all. Just get enough information for a report and get the hell out of there. You want to take it as slow as the situation allows. Over time I've read a lot of stories in journals, stories picked up in the news, war stories at conferences, all about officers that went on calls to which solutions should have been easily found but ended up in physical confrontations that led to fatal consequences. In seventy percent of the cases, I read or heard about, situations escalated because of the approach, ego or actions of the responding officer. You want a good example of the wrong approach? Here's one. You are sent on a call, "Man threatening people with a knife"." When you arrive on scene, you identify a young man at a stand off with several people, they're keeping a safe distance from him and he's yelling and screaming at the group and holding a knife in a threatening way. The first thing responding officers do is pull their weapons and all of them start screaming, **Put the knife down, Drop the knife, Drop the knife, on your knees,** or some other threatening command, instead of one of the officers calmly communicating with the person, while the rest of the team clear the area. Instead, the individual is facing a bunch of guns pointing at him by people yelling and hollering at him from all directions. A perfect scenario to make the person want to escape. If he runs, somebody will probably shoot, and put a bullet in the suspects back. Hear me!! There is almost no excuse for putting a bullet in a person's back! Now I grew up on a ranch and I've seen hands scream and holler, hanging on to a horse with a two by four in their hands. The muscles of that animal tighten up and quiver, all of its weight goes to its hind legs. It's frightened, and its preparing to defend itself or try to get away. The same thing is happening to the man with the knife and he'll probably do something stupid and get shot. A little patience and calmness de-escalates the situation, the knifer realizes what a precarious situation he's in and begins to calm down. Now the chances of getting him to drop the knife have increased. Unfortunately there will be those cases where other actions may be required. Remember that there is strength in numbers which tends to reduce the probability that action taken will have to be lethal. Taking a life should never be your first option unless your life or the life of another is in eminent danger." Again, Craig paused to sip water from the glass on the podium. Over the glass he observed the group. They were sitting upright in their seats and appeared to be just waiting for him to go on. He was sure they had heard what he said before but maybe not in the same way. He started again.

"The third chapter in that soft covered book was **Understanding** and **Compassion**. There are five reasons a citizen calls a police officer. Number one they're scared. A situation has them scared that they or somebody else is gonna get hurt or somebody is bad hurt. Second they're angry. Somebody in some way has taken advantage of em or their property; some body's not controlling their kids or animals; or somebody has taken something from them, a burglary or a theft. Third, there's been an accident and they are involved one way or another; Fourth, there has been an unattended death and fifth, they just need somebody to talk to. In either case, they perceive their situation to be serious and a little understanding and a bunch of compassion can go a long way. The next chapter had to do with **attitude**. Don't let your ego get in the way of getting the job done. Everyone is not happy to see you when you appear on the scene. Instant compliance with your instructions, though desired, may not happen. keep your ego in check, don't become a part of the problem, let persons know that your intent is to help. If situations are unstable, take charge without causing things to escalate. If things are relatively calm, keep them that way. In most cases, people don't want you to solve their problems, they want someone to help them find a solution that they can live with, and you're it. The last chapter was **Discretion**. That's a fancy word for common sense. The leadership of most law enforcement agencies allow its officers a certain amount of reasonable discretion. Remember the individual driving under the influence? The reason he or she got your attention in the first place probably, is because they made a left turn with the right turn signal blinking; or the guy making an ass of himself in one of the local drinking establishments? Rather than take the drunk to jail, he hasn't done anything reckless so as to hurt anyone, why not let him or her call somebody to come drive them home; and the disorderly person causing a disturbance, hasn't hurt anybody, hasn't caused damage to property, doesn't appear to be drunk, just being an ass. Why not take him out of the place and send his butt on his way? There is a delicate situation that you're bound to face and that's the domestic disturbance. I believe it's the most dangerous call a police officer can go to. You never know how its going to turn out. Either of the combatants can turn on you. First rule: If at all possible, never go to such a call by yourself. Second rule: Upon arrival separate the combatants into different areas. Third rule: Only one officer interview while the other makes sure the combatants stay away from one another and you. Rule four – There is no rule four. You're on your own now. Unless one party files a complaint against the other, you'll probably leave them where they can get at each other again. You then have to hope your skill at delivering a stern warning, is enough to prevent you from having to come back and maybe your calmness in handling things had helped to defuse the situation, then you keep your fingers crossed. Sometimes you may be able to convince one of the parties to spend time with a relative or friend until things cool down. In such situations **respect, patience, understanding and compassion, attitude and discretion** is gonna save your bacon. There's something else I'll leave with you. Get to know the people in your community or better yet, let the people in your community get to know you." Craig turned to the podium, picked up his hat and put it on so that it rested to the back of his head and spoke again to the group.

"I have not tried to tell you what a **police officer** is today. You learned that in this academy. What you heard today from me is how to be a **Peace Officer**. What worked for me over the years, hopefully, will work for you too." With that craig walked into the audience and shook the hand of each person and wished them luck. Returning to the front he shook Carl's hand and thanked him for the invite. There was thunderous applause and a standing ovation as Craig left the building. After dismissing the group Carl joined Craig outside.

"You know, I've been through a few of these graduations, but I don't think I've heard anyone address graduates from that angle," Carl said as he shook Craigs hand.

"You think maybe," Craig began with a big grin on his face. "It's because your speakers have always been people still in the business instead of leaving it. I'm sure there is a different prospective and I wanted to give those people things to think about that they can't find in textbooks and manuals. Well Carl, it's a long way back to Green River and I best be heading that way. Nice meeting you and again, thanks for the invite." Craig tipped his hat and slid behind the wheel of his 1970's Chrysler and eased out on highway 191 to highway I-80 and headed south west. During some of the Four and a half hours of travel Craig pictured the faces of the graduating class in his mind and wondered, will they or won't they be able to give what the job demands. Will they or won't they remember that their job is to serve and not to judge; to protect and not execute except as a last resort.

The sun was low in the western sky, it would soon be dusk, and he looked forward to seeing the sunset. He saw the white rear ends of the antelope that gathered, grazing in the fields on both sides of the road, and after some time a deer with a magnificent rack crossed the road some distance in front of him and rabbits scampered down the edge of the highway caught in the cars headlights as darkness fell, and he smiled and thought, *Wyoming-What a great place to live.*

THE END

CHARACTERS

Craig Spence	Sheriff Sweetwater County
Martha Spence	Wife – Mrs. Craig Spence
Sherrie Mullins	Jail Administrator
Steve Lolly	First Deputy
Kevin Marcy	Chief Detective
Harry Kushner	Deputy Sheriff
Sarah Cousins	County Attorney
Nancy	Receptionist at County Attorney's Office
Raul	County Commissioner
Matt Kessler	Rock Springs Chief of Police
Pappy Masters	Rock Springs PD Detective
Lt Tobias	Supervisor, rock Springs PD
Clinton Tucker	Police Officer
Candice Tucker	Mother-Clinton Tucker
Tina Morgan	Clinton Tuckers Sister
Mr. Morris	School Principal
Ed Rosenberg	Pawnshop Owner
Strome Cooper	Ed's Buddy
Peter Stricker	District Judge
Jack Abramoff	Elections Commissioner
Carl Christensen	Director Police Academy

Sergeant Kravitz	Jail supervisor in Evanston
Paul Mason	Owner-Crystal Pistol
Jess Preston	Drug Dealer
Anne Stoffer	Crystal Pistol Bookkeeper
Tom Paxton	Crystal Pistol Lead Bar tender
Pete Lomas	Bar tender
Carla Denton	Cocktail Waitress
Marta Preston	Cocktail Waitress
Missy Parker	Food Server
Dan Denton	Food Server
Max Munson	Cook
Mammy Title	Cook
Kaylee	Abandoned Child
Clarice	Woman Mentally Challenged

Other Books

— By —

JR Conway

GREYHOUND THERAPY: *People move from place to place for any number of reasons. It was always intriguing to look at people and try to imagine why they were on the bus, where they were coming from or where they might be going. In some cases, people with health or mental problems were given bus tickets by law enforcement agencies and put on the bus to get them out of their jurisdictions. Craig Spence, Sheriff of Sweetwater County, WY. Was the recipient of some of this migration. The author takes the reader on a fast- paced journey of crime fighting and life changing experiences*

AFTER THE RIDE: *Often, persons damaged by war are set afloat in an environment in which they are no longer equipped to function, and they occasionally became wards of Sheriff Craig Spence. After The Ride describes just such an occasion that leads Sheriff Spence on a marathon effort to investigate and crack a major crime enterprise.*

CRAIG SPENCE-SHERIFF: *Sweetwater County*, Wyoming was going through an oil and gas boom and people were converging on the small communities of Green River and Rock Springs, looking to take advantage of high dollar jobs. The populations exploded and Craig Spence, Sheriff of Sweetwater County, was tasked with applying the law in a different manner. Craig Spence was not your run of the mill lawman, he thought outside the box and he brought humane methods to enforcement.